TO SEE AND KNOW

Margo Hauser

MARGO HANSEN

TO SEE AND KNOW

All Scripture quotations in this book are taken from the King James Version of the Bible.

This novel is a work of fiction. Names, descriptions, entities, and incidents included in the story are products of the author's imagination. Any resemblance to actual persons, events, and entities is entirely coincidental.

To See and Know
    Copyright © 2019 by Margo Hansen.
All rights reserved.
    ISBN-13: 978-1694638212

Published in the United States of America

1. Fiction / Action & Adventure
2. Fiction / Christian / Historical Romance

In memory of
my grandparents:
Ma and Pa
(Olive and Palmer Stende)

And
my grandpa:
Millard Nygaard

To the people of Ulen,
who still have a proud,
pioneering spirit and
respect for their land

To my husband Bruce,
who lights my way

Acknowledgments

My thanks to my mom, Marilyn (Stende) Nygaard, for giving me more details of Ulen's history including the story of my grandmother, Olive (Purrier) Stende, who as a young girl had to drive the family surrey through the town and nearly got in an accident. I added her story near the end of *To See and Know* and only changed one detail by letting one of my characters step in to help. I was also thrilled to mention my great-grandfather, John Stende, as the mailman and owner of the livery.

It has been fun to include some of Ulen's history into my fictional story. I again give credit to my late aunt, Eldora (Stende) Lunde, and the others who compiled the information in *Spanning the Century, the History of Ulen, Minnesota*. Besides reporting the struggles of the pioneers who settled the area with stories of droughts, fires, hailstorms, windstorms, blizzards, cyclones, and grasshopper invasions, they added the humorous stories of the man who moved his barn to the middle of the street because of a surveyor's error, the man who defended himself in a hold-up by hitting the robber with a piece of dried beef, and the man in jail for stealing a bear, just to mention a few.

Many thanks to my readers who, after reading *A Sweet Voice* have written me such wonderful letters and emails about their own experiences in the Ulen area. It has been a blessing to me to make new friends and to renew relationships with relatives who knew me when I was very young. I hope you will enjoy this sequel as well.

Many, many thanks to my daughters Megan and Brooke for your honest critiques as you read my manuscripts and offer suggestions. I appreciate you so much.

And, thanks to my husband Bruce, whose encouragement is priceless.

Preface

The town of Ulen, Minnesota, is uniquely located being equidistance from the Gulf of Mexico and Hudson Bay, Canada, and it lies midway between the Atlantic and Pacific Oceans, placing it nearly in the center of North America.

Between the years 1893 and 1913 the town had become quite modernized. Electricity, the Model T, gas tractors, and a telephone system were highlights of the times. An orchestra, a baseball team, a girls' basketball team, a creamery association, the Ladies' Aid, a bowling alley, and movies at the Opera House added to social life. About 95% of the population were Norwegians.

Ulen's famous Viking Sword was discovered by Hans O. Hanson in 1911, while plowing his field. It is believed to be about 500 years old. The sword is on display at the Ulen Museum.

World and national events leading up to 1913 included Teddy Roosevelt charging up San Juan Hill, the last Indian uprising in the nation near Leech Lake, MN, the assassination of President McKinley, the building of the Panama Canal, the flight of the Wright Brothers, the San Francisco earthquake, and the sinking of the Titanic.

That the God of our Lord Jesus Christ, the Father of glory, may give unto you the spirit of wisdom and revelation in the knowledge of him:
The eyes of your understanding being enlightened; that ye may know what is the hope of his calling, and what the riches of the glory of his inheritance in the saints,
And what is the exceeding greatness of his power to us-ward who believe, according to the working of his mighty power,
Which he wrought in Christ, when he raised him from the dead, and set him at his own right hand in the heavenly places,

Ephesians 1:17-20

Keane and Tuva Wheatly

Torkel
Melody
Harmony
Aslak
Tobias

Jake and Mina Rodwell

Josiah
Eve
Aaron
Naomi

one

1898

"Why are we stopping here, Mother?"

Ten-year-old Garrett followed his mother down the train steps onto the platform. The dark-haired boy tugged at the collar of the jacket his mother insisted he wore. He was sweltering in the heat, not only from standing beside the train, but also because it was a very hot August day. He stood by his mother's side while she looked around her as if she were searching for something. She gave her son no reply but took his hand and walked toward one of the men from the train. Garrett didn't hear what she asked the man as he was distracted by the sight of the small depot. People had gathered to see the newcomers get off the train and some were bidding farewell to others boarding it. They looked nothing like the people in the city where he had lived. The men wore mostly bib overalls and the women simple skirts and blouses or cotton dresses. His mother walked slowly by them, which was good because it gave Garrett more time to look around. He was as curious about the people in this small town as they seemed to be about the travelers.

He had been asleep on the train until it slowed and the screeching of the brakes woke him. Out the window he saw open prairie for miles and miles, and the sign post by the tracks claimed their station was Ulen and boasted a population of over three hundred residents.

"Are we still in North Dakota, Mother?"

His mother glanced down at her son and Garrett saw weariness in her face. "No, this is Minnesota. Come along now." She put a hand on his shoulder to guide him to walk with her.

Garrett tried to hear what the people at the station were talking about as they walked past, but he could only hear snippets of what they were saying.

"Seven people were killed in that uprising! If it happened at Leech Lake, it can happen here."

"There was no need to move the depot. It was just fine two blocks from here. I declare…"

"The Rough Riders took care of Cuba. I see great things for Roosevelt's future."

"It's so hot again! I heard it was 111° yesterday. Just think, last year Fargo was flooded."

The conversations drifted away as Garrett and his mother descended the platform and began walking down the town's street. Garrett looked from one side to the other, his face revealing his astonishment. They passed the City Hall and jail, a saloon, the Stebbin's House, which appeared to be a hotel, and something called Cook and Kankel's Roller Mill.

Garrett slowed as he tried to read some of the signs, but his mother pulled him along. Besides the livery and blacksmith, a wagon shop and bank, he saw Austinson & Asleson's General Store. They passed another hotel and he spied women's hats in the window. He realized they were leaving the town when he had to look over his shoulder to see the last building.

"Are there Indians here? Someone said there was an uprising! Where are we going? What is this place anyway? I've never seen such a small town." Garrett's mother stopped abruptly and stared at something in front of them. He looked up at her in puzzlement before turning to see where she was looking. Before them was a small cemetery. He frowned and looked again to his mother for explanation, but she began moving among the headstones, glancing at each one then passing by.

Garrett dropped her hand and followed at his own pace. Nothing was making sense. They had been traveling for days on their way to Chicago, and this was the first time they got off the train to walk around. Why did his mother want to walk through a cemetery? What was she looking for? Who was she looking for?

He watched her go from grave to grave, giving a negative shake of her head after reading each one. She looked around and Garrett could see her bite at her lower lip. She only did that when something was troubling her. Sometimes he wondered if she'd have a lip left after all the trouble they'd been through, but she always managed to solve their problems. The thing is that he didn't know what the problem was this time. Her head lifted slightly and Garrett followed her gaze. There was a grave a little apart from the others, and she headed for it.

As he followed his mother, Garrett heard voices behind him. Turning, he saw a woman with two little girls approach a grave, so he paused to watch them. The woman was carrying flowers, yellow and orange ones, and she placed them in front of a stone. She was a tall woman and her blonde hair was braided like a crown on her head. The two little girls wore their blonde braids down their backs. The woman was talking to the girls, one whom Garrett guessed to be about five years old and the other younger. He moved on toward his mother but kept sneaking glances back at the trio. The older girl placed her hands on the top of the grave stone and slid them down either side then she traced the name on the stone with her finger. As odd as that looked to Garrett, he was stunned when they started singing. He had reached his mother's side by this time and together they stared at the three of them singing a song unknown to Garrett. It was the most beautiful sound he had ever heard.

"Time to go, girls." He heard the woman say. "Melody, take Harmony's hand. We'll stop by the store before we go home."

The woman smiled at Garrett as she passed by and she nodded to his mother, but she didn't speak, and Garrett felt his mother was relieved by that. The little girls followed their mother and the youngest one waved her free hand at Garrett. As she did so, she tripped on a rock, but her sister kept her from falling.

"Harmony, you need to look where you're going." The older girl told her.

Garrett watched as they left the cemetery before he turned to see what his mother had found, but she was already moving on. He followed her past a few more stones, but it seemed her interest in them was gone.

"We'll stay the night at one of the hotels and leave in the morning," she announced.

Garrett held his hands palms up. "But why did we come here? Did you know someone who died in this town?"

His mother stopped and turned to Garrett. She looked him in the eye as she slid her knuckles down the side of his cheek. She always did that, and though he never told her so, he kind of liked it.

"Yes, dear. I knew someone long ago and I just wanted to stop to say a last goodbye."

"Is it someone I knew?"

She sighed a little before she smiled sadly. "No. It's no one you knew."

1913 ~ Fifteen Years Later

Melody Wheatly wasn't aware of the man in the cemetery when she made her way to her grandparents' graves. She stood in front of her grandfather's first and placed her hands on the headstone and let them slide down the sides. Then she traced his name with her finger. *Thane Wheatly.* She kissed her fingers and lightly touched the stone before moving to the one beside it. She did the same with that one. *Wilhelmina Wheatly.* She lingered a bit longer there, whispering, "I miss you so much, Grandma." A bird unexpectedly fluttered into the air and Melody turned her head to the sound. She stood very still for a few seconds as if listening then she moved through the graveyard and made her way toward town.

Garrett Foxe watched the young lady with interest. Fifteen years hadn't dulled his memory in the least. He remembered every detail of the day he and his mother stopped in the farming community of Ulen, Minnesota, so he knew by her actions that this was the very same girl who had been in the cemetery that day long ago. Her blonde hair was braided down her back just as it had been back then too. He waited until the young woman was out of sight before he stepped from behind the branches of the young tree where he had hid while he watched her, and he wondered if the bird he had scared into flight had alerted her to his presence even though she gave no indication of seeing him there. Hiding had been a natural instinct. He wasn't ready to let anyone know who he was or why he was there. He glanced down again at the gravestone he had come to see and took a deep breath. Every word on it was etched in his mind just as it was etched in the stone before him.

He looked down the road again. Seeing no one about, he stepped over to the graves where the girl had stood. The first time he had been there only one stone existed. Now there were two. He read the names and his lips tightened. The date of death on the second one was only three years previous. The names meant nothing to him, but the fact that they were important to the young lady piqued his interest. It shouldn't have felt odd to him that she was there as he supposed she made a regular habit of visiting the graves of some relatives, but the fact that he had come to the graveyard the same time she did fifteen years later gave him an unsettling feeling.

He decided to follow the girl back to town. He knew no one here, a town as strange and unfamiliar to him as it had been when he briefly saw it as a boy, but this girl, the one he had seen when she was but a child, was the only familiar person to him. Maybe she would have some answers for him.

Her walking speed surprised him. Her stride was purposeful and she never looked to the right or left as she made her way back to town. He stayed a distance from her, not wanting her to know he was behind her. He'd catch up to her in town and introduce himself and strike up a conversation. But when the lady approached the buildings of town, she stopped and called out, "Harmony!"

Garrett slowed his steps, puzzled by the girl's behavior. A man who had been loading a wagon hurried over to the girl and spoke to her. Taking her arm he led her to the mercantile where another young lady was just exiting.

"Here's Harmony, Melody." He heard the man say. "Everything okay now?"

"Yes, thanks, Jasper."

The girl called Harmony leaned close to hear what the other was saying. Garrett was startled when she turned and looked directly at him as if accusing him of something. Had the girl been aware of him behind her the whole way? Was she afraid of him? But why?

The ladies moved on down the street, their arms linked. They didn't turn back again. He was so bewildered by their behavior that he wasn't aware of the man who approached him, the one from the wagon.

"Why are you following Melody?"

"What? I'm not—"

"You got business with her, you talk to me."

"What? I don't have business—"

"Hey there, Ole, what seems to be the trouble?"

Garrett looked over his shoulder as another man, an older one, wearing a butcher's apron, was speaking again to the young man who had approached Garrett.

"That's no way to treat a guest in our town, Ole." Looking at Garrett, the man held out his hand. "Hello. Name's Ole Asleson and this here's Ole Jasperson. Welcome to Ulen."

Garrett shook the hand. "Garrett Foxe. Look, I'm sorry if I startled the lady. I wasn't following her." He glanced first at one man and then at the other.

"No, of course not. Ole here is just over protective of Melody."

The man called Ole Jasperson, wore dusty overalls over his bare, tanned arms. He grunted as if in disgust. "And Ole here is always butting in where he doesn't belong." Then, startling Garrett even further, he grinned and slapped the older man on the back.

Relaxing a bit at the turn of events, Garrett ventured a comment. "Must get confusing having the same name."

Ole Asleson replied first. "We call this guy Jasper just so's folks don't get us too confused. 'Course there were our founders Ole Ulen and Ole Odneland, and our neighbor Ole Melbye, but we keep 'em all straight. Now, what can I do for you, young feller?"

"Uh, well, I just got into town and…uh…well, I'm kind of looking for work."

"Ah!" Ole stroked his chin as he eyed the stranger then quirked an eyebrow in Jasper's direction. "There's usually work to be found 'round harvest time. I'll put the word out that you're looking. Not afraid of some hard labor, are you?"

"No, sir. I don't know much about farming, but I'm not afraid of work."

"Okay then. Stop by the mercantile over there tomorrow and I'll let you know what I find out."

"Thank you, Mr. Asleson." Garrett shook the man's hand and tipped his hat to the man called Jasper. As he walked away, the two men watched him. It was Ole Asleson who spoke first.

"That feller looks familiar, like someone I've seen before."

Jasper grunted again. "I don't care what he looks like. He just better leave Melody alone."

Ole faced the farmer. "You know, Jasper, Melody's a grown woman now. She doesn't need you looking out for her anymore."

"Ain't none of your business." Jasper walked back to his wagon, leaving the storekeeper to his thoughts.

"Just seems like I've seen that feller somewhere before." Ole stroked his chin again and headed back to his store.

Melody squeezed her sister's arm. "Of course I'm all right, just a little embarrassed is all. Leave it to Jasper to come to my rescue. You go ahead and finish your shopping. I know my way home."

Harmony leaned her head on Melody's shoulder. "Sometimes I wonder if I'm doing the right thing, taking on a school in Flom and leaving you."

Melody stopped walking so abruptly that Harmony was caught off balance. "That's the most ridiculous thing I've ever heard,

Harmony Wheatly! You make me sound like an invalid needing a keeper. Well, I've never asked for—"

"I know, I know. Sorry. Melody, you're the most independent woman I know. Maybe it's me I'm thinking of who needs a keeper." She patted the hand on her arm. "I'm going to miss my time with you this winter."

Melody laughed. "It's not like you're going away very far. Dad will come get you for the weekends until the snow prevents travel. Besides, I'll be busy helping the teacher here again this year, so we wouldn't see much of each other anyway. Now, go. I'll see you back at home."

Melody hugged Harmony and strode away, knowing full well that her sister watched her go. She felt the heat of the August sun on her back and could feel the softness of the grass just alongside the road as she walked. The grass helped only a little in keeping the dirt off her clothing, and it mattered even less when a wagon went by and covered her in a cloud of dust. She enjoyed the freedom she felt when walking the country roads. She knew every pace by heart, every farm driveway she passed, and every mailbox she counted. She could tell a bird or an insect by its song and knew the name of each flower whose fragrance reached her nostrils.

But her mind wandered from her surroundings to the person who had been in the cemetery. Normally on a visit to her grandparents' graves she would sing one of their favorite hymns. She knew her beloved Ma and Pa weren't there to hear her; they were enjoying heaven with their Savior. Still, the song and visit gave her comfort and reminded her of the joy her grandparents were to her. It had become a tradition ever since she was a child, but today she refrained from singing because she was aware of someone else there. If it had been someone from town, they would have greeted her, and they all knew of her visits and left her alone, but this person didn't make himself known. She hadn't even known it was a man until Harmony told her. She had walked swiftly back to town without waiting to find out, a little niggling sense of fear creeping up the back of her neck as she did so.

The creak of a wagon caused her to turn her head. *That will be Jasper.* Melody stopped and waited alongside the road until the wagon came to a stop beside her.

"Want a ride, Melody?" Jasper's friendly voice always made her smile. He was eleven years her senior, but he had been her champion and friend all through her growing up years and especially those trying days at school when she had felt alone and afraid of the unknown. It was Jasper who protected her from the bullies and the pranks of other students. He was their nearest neighbor now, and a ride home with him made sense, but today she wanted to be alone.

"Hi Jasper. No thanks, I'm enjoying the walk today."

"Okay."

The wagon didn't move and Melody waited.

"That feller is new in town and looking for work. I don't think he was following you."

"Thank you. Guess it just made me nervous."

"You know, Melody—"

"You better get going, Jasper. That butter will melt in this heat."

"How do you know I got butter?"

Melody laughed. "You think I can't smell Mrs. Johanson's homemade rolls in that bag beside you? When you buy those, you buy butter."

"And how do you know I have a bag beside me?"

Melody cocked her head to one side. "Because you slid it closer to you when you offered me a ride."

"Melody Wheatly, you beat all. If a person didn't know no better, they'd never know you was blind."

The trill of Melody's laughter caused nearby birds to take flight and break into song. "We need to work on your grammar, Jasper. I declare it's gotten worse the older you get. And you're getting mighty old now. Over thirty, aren't you?"

Jasper grunted. "Just for that, you go on and walk yourself home. You ain't gettin' no ride from me."

The wagon creaked as the man on the seat slapped the reins. Melody's laughter followed it as she continued on her way. Blind as she was, she could still see what a great friend she had in Jasper. She smiled as she recalled the stories her mother and Mina used to tell about young Ole Jasperson and his escapades. He even caught the bouquet at her parents' wedding.

Then the smile faded as she thought again about her experience in the cemetery. She was rarely frightened by anything, not allowing her blindness to keep her from living a *normal* life, but the feeling of someone watching her was so unsettling that she had panicked.

It's not as if you aren't used to being watched, she grudgingly reminded herself. If it wasn't someone in her family, it was Jasper who kept an eye on her. They were a comforting part of her life, but this stranger had a far different effect on her. One that she was having trouble shaking.

two

It had been a stressful day. Garrett sank back on the bed in his hotel room, his arm across his forehead. He came to this town for answers, but the questions were multiplying and not all had to do with his reason for being here.

Why was that girl afraid of him? She hadn't even looked his way as far as he knew, so why did she take off like a scared rabbit? He had hoped to approach her and glean some information about the town from her, but her rapid departure had put a halt to that. And why did she call out when she was in the middle of the street? Didn't she know where her friend was? Did people in this town just yell out a name when they wanted someone? And the girl who joined her. Why did she turn and give him an accusing stare?

That guy practically threatened him to leave the girl alone. What was that all about? At least the storekeeper was friendly and had put him on to a possible job. What was expected of him on a farm? He had no idea, but it couldn't be any worse than some of the jobs he had undertaken ever since he was eight years old.

Answers. That's what he needed.

He got up and poured water from the pitcher into the wash bowl and splashed his face and neck. The day was warm and humid, and he felt a clean shirt was necessary before going downstairs for his supper. He combed his black hair back, noting he was in need of a haircut soon, but he'd have to watch his spending until he got some income. He used up a good sum just getting here and for all he knew, it could all be for naught.

The next day he entered the mercantile as soon as it opened and waited until the owner was free.

"Mr. Foxe!" Ole Asleson shook the young man's hand. "I checked around for you and there's not much at the moment, but in another week or so harvest will begin and then there will surely be work."

"Another week?"

Something in the man's voice made the storekeeper pause.

"If you don't mind being indoors, I could use some help the next few days going over my inventory."

Garrett's face brightened. "Yes, sir. I mean, no, sir, I don't mind being indoors or outdoors or whatever."

"Okay then. Follow me and I'll get you started."

"Thank you, sir."

Garrett suspected that the man was making up the job as a charitable gesture, but at this point, he didn't care. He needed some money just to survive staying at the hotel and getting one meal a day. It was something he was used to, this scrimping to get by. After getting some answers and some income, he'd move on and get a real job somewhere and hopefully begin a life of his own.

Ole had Garrett count items and write quantities down. It was more involved than Garrett realized. Never before had he been in a store with such a variety of goods. There were food items like canned goods, rounds of cheese and crocks of pickles. There was flour in sacks and coffee beans and herring in brine. There were some things he had never heard of before.

"Uh, Ole, what kind of berries are in these pails?"

"Those are lingonberries."

"Okay, and, sir, what's that?"

Ole looked up from figuring his books. He grinned at Garrett. "Those are dried slabs of lutefisk. Come Christmas you won't find any left in stock. You ever had lutefisk, Garrett?"

"No, but I'll try anything."

The storekeeper chuckled to himself and went back to his work.

Garrett moved on. Jugs of vinegar sat on the floor next to jugs of kerosene. Tools lined shelves, some familiar to him, others things he had heard of but never used. Clothing and material stacked up nearby. He saw bib overalls like Ole Jasperson had on and blue work shirts next to women's hats and baby things. Sewing items and cooking utensils and chewing tobacco swam before his eyes.

Ole slapped the account book shut and walked over to where Garrett was working. "We measure out the flour and coffee beans by the pound. Women often bring in their eggs or some ham or butter in exchange for groceries or goods, so the bookkeeping gets a bit complicated."

"I see." Garrett was amazed.

The storekeeper looked over Garrett's shoulder at the notebook he was writing in. "A lot of people can't afford to pay for their goods until after harvest, so I just keep lots of records. What you're doing there is a big help to me. I haven't had time to check on inventory."

"I'm glad to help." Garrett finished writing in the notebook then looked up. "You must know all the people around here."

"I sure do. Someone you're looking for? Oh, excuse me, I have a customer."

Garrett turned to the door and saw the young lady who had come out of the mercantile when the woman he followed called out her name. *Harmony, wasn't it?* He listened to Ole greet her.

"Good morning, Miss Wheatly, what can I do for you today?"

Wheatly. That was the name on the headstones in the cemetery.

"Morning, Mr. Asleson. I'd like to look at the fabric, please. I'm going to need a couple more dresses if I'm going to be a schoolteacher." Garrett saw her smile at the man and though she hadn't yet seen Garrett, he found himself smiling at her. She had blonde hair like the girl named Melody, and today it was pinned up with lots of loose curls scattered about her face. She was quite lovely, and he was staring at her when she turned and saw him. Her face changed from welcoming to suspicious.

"I have some new fabric in, Harmony. Come take a look. Oh, this is Garrett Foxe. I think you saw him yesterday. Garrett, this is Harmony Wheatly. She's going to teach school in Flom this year."

"How do you do?" Garrett hoped his smile would invoke a more friendly response from the girl than what she was showing.

"Hello." Harmony gave him a nod then moved to look at the fabric. Garrett continued with his work and was aware that she gave him cursory glances. He was surprised when she spoke to him again.

"Are you working here?"

"Yes, Mr. Asleson is having me do the inventory for him. I hope to get a job helping someone with harvesting soon, although truthfully I don't know what that means." He smiled again and was finally rewarded with a smile in return.

Then Harmony's smile faded as if she remembered something. Her next words startled him. "Melody doesn't like to be followed."

"Oh. Yes…well…I didn't mean to frighten her. I was in the cemetery too, and I just left the same time she did, I guess. I'm very sorry that my actions scared her. Uh, is she your sister?"

"Yes."

Harmony went back to fingering the fabrics, but kept looking over at Garrett. She seemed as curious about him, as he was about her.

"Are you staying in Ulen?"

"Yes, I'm over at the Orient Hotel."

"No, I mean, are you staying…are you going to live here?"

"Uh, I don't know yet. I'm actually looking for—"

A man entering the store interrupted their conversation. "Harmony! Are you ready yet? I've loaded supplies."

"Almost, Dad. Excuse me," she said to Garrett. She brought some rolls of fabric to the storekeeper and told him the amounts she wanted. While she waited for the fabric to be cut, she conversed with the man who stood beside her, whom Garrett assumed was her father. As they were preparing to leave, Garrett walked to the counter.

"Good day, Miss Wheatly. It was nice to meet you." He nodded to the man. For just a moment Garrett thought the man was going to speak to him, but when he didn't Garrett stepped back into one of the aisles and continued with his work.

"Dad?" Harmony took her father's arm and started for the door. "Dad, is something wrong?"

Keane Wheatly shook his head as if to clear it. He looked down at his daughter. "No, honey. Ready?"

Garrett didn't get a chance to talk to his employer the rest of the day as customers kept the man busy. There were questions he needed to ask that would help him decide his future. He had to start somewhere and this was the place that seemed to hold the answers.

Ever since his mother died and he had found the papers she had hid from him, he had been holding in his anger and his unbelief. He needed to sort things out so he could decide where his life would go from here.

The next day was Sunday and the store was closed. Ole invited Garrett to attend his church, which was a few miles northeast of town. Garrett was undecided until the man mentioned that Harmony Wheatly also attended there. He wondered if the storekeeper had seen his interest in the girl because interested he was. Perhaps going to the church would give him an opportunity to visit with the people and get some questions answered.

Since the small country church was a distance from town, he rented a buggy. He heard the singing before he reached the door and realized he was late, so he slipped in the door and sat in the back. The preacher sat in a chair to the left of the pulpit while a man stood directing the congregation in singing. At the piano, much to Garrett's surprise, was the young woman from the cemetery. Her profile was toward the people, and Garrett could see that she played without the benefit of music. Her fingers danced over the keys making melodies that caused Garrett to close his eyes in appreciation. He reluctantly opened his eyes when the singing stopped and almost missed the announcement of a special song, but when three women approached the podium, they got his immediate attention. One was the girl from the piano, the other was Harmony Wheatly, but it was the older woman with braided blonde hair that caused him to stare. He remembered her. She was the one at the cemetery fifteen years earlier with the two little girls—these girls—who had to be her daughters.

For the next several minutes Garrett sat mesmerized by the blending of the three voices singing without accompaniment. He closed his eyes and let the music pour into him. He was completely entranced by the sound of the song and then he began to hear the words:

> *Souls in danger, look above,*
> *Jesus completely saves;*
> *He will lift you by His love*
> *Out of the angry waves,*
> *He's the Master of the sea,*
> *Billows His will obey;*
> *He your Savior wants to be—*
> *Be saved today.*
>
> *Love lifted me! Love lifted me!*
> *When nothing else could help,*
> *Love lifted me.*
> *Love lifted me! Love lifted me!*
> *When nothing else could help,*
> *Love lifted me.*

The ladies stepped down and returned to their seats and the preacher took the pulpit. There was a smile on his face as he turned the pages in the Bible before him.

"Thank you, Tuva, Melody, and Harmony for introducing us to another new hymn. As many of you know of my past, you will understand why this song has touched my soul. The words of the first verse explain it well: *But the Master of the sea heard my despairing cry, from the waters lifted me, now safe am I.*

"It was over twenty years ago that the Lord rescued Keane Wheatly and me from the angry waves and the bonds of slavery. More importantly he rescued us from the slavery of sin through his abundant love. It was his love for us and for each of you that made him willingly go to the cross to die for our sins. Forgiveness is ours when we place our trust in him, when we believe that he did it for us, that he rose from the dead, that he loves us now and forever. Let's open our Bibles to the book of Romans, if you please."

Garrett sat transfixed by the words of the preacher. This was something he had never heard before. His heart started beating faster. For so much of his life he felt lost like he was adrift at sea with no purpose or destination. The message he was hearing was offering him hope that there was more to life than just getting through one day only to face another. He soaked up the words, wishing he had a Bible in front of him to see them for himself.

His eyes never left the preacher's face as he continued to expound God's grace to all in his message. Then the preacher looked directly at him, and the words stopped. Garrett waited, confused by the shocked expression on the man's face. Something was wrong. The people began turning around to see what had caught their pastor's attention, and Garrett became uneasy. He ducked his head and quietly got up and left the building. He was in the buggy and headed down the road when he heard a voice behind him call out, "Wait!" But he kept going. Something was very wrong and that something was because of him. He needed to know what it was, but not now. Not with the frightened look on that preacher's face haunting him. He had to get away.

Jake Rodwell stunned his congregation when he ran down the aisle and chased after the man who slipped out the door. He stood on the road watching the buggy race away and tried to steady his breathing. He heard the people singing behind him and was thankful that the song leader took over, but he couldn't take his eyes off the road.

A hand gripped his shoulder. "I told you. It was him, wasn't it?"

Jake turned to Keane. He shook his head. "But it can't be."

"I thought my heart stopped when I saw him at the mercantile the other day. I know you told me I was seeing things, but it's true."

The men stood in silence, each in their own thoughts, until Jake spoke again. "Thorpe is dead, Keane. We both know it. This guy just looks uncannily like him. Nothing more."

"Jake!"

"There's Mina. She's going to think I've gone crazy." He patted Keane on the back. "I've got to go shake hands and try to explain what just happened. Let's talk later, okay?"

"Sure, Jake."

Jake took his place beside his wife at the door of the church and bid the churchgoers a good day. He laughed off his strange behavior and teased that they all got out a lot earlier because of it.

After most of the people had started down the road to their homes, Mina turned to Jake. "What was that all about?"

Jake checked that their four children were standing by the family surrey. He lowered his voice to speak to his wife. "That man in the back looked just like Thorpe."

Mina's mouth dropped open as she stared at her husband. "No!" Then, "Jake, could he have had a son? He must have had a son!" She turned to look down the dirt road. "But why is he here? How would he know to come here?"

"Maybe…" Jake hesitated to say it, but he knew what his wife was thinking. "Maybe…revenge."

"What made your father race down the aisle like that, Josiah? I've never seen him do anything like that in a church service before."

Torkel stood beside the family's surrey with his brothers and Melody and Harmony and the Rodwell children.

"I have no idea. I never saw that guy before, but he sure took off out of there."

"Well, I would too if Pa started chasing after me." Aaron exclaimed.

"That's 'cuz he's chased you down a time or two when you've gotten yourself in trouble." Naomi laughed at her brother.

Melody listened, one hand on the surrey so she was out of the way of the people milling about. She was very comfortable in familiar surroundings and with people who watched out for her, but in crowds she was better off staying in one spot. She chafed at times, having her brothers Torkel, Aslak, and Tobias or her sister Harmony lead her about, but she had learned that it was her pride that made her feel that way. It had been a hard lesson to learn because she was independent by nature, but she knew her family loved her and wanted to protect her. Her four siblings and the four Rodwell children were her dearest friends. Their parents had a bond that went back to the time when Pastor Jake and her father Keane had been held as shanghaied prisoners on a ship and had escaped together. The two men had become like brothers and the families as if they were related. And now they would be with the upcoming marriage of her older brother Torkel to Jake and Mina's daughter and her closest friend Eve.

Melody was delighted that Torkel and Eve would marry. Eventually the couple would build a house, but for now they would move into the little house on the same property as the Wheatlys, left vacant after her grandparents' passing. Her father and Jake had built the house when Tuva and Keane married, so that the larger home would be for the younger couple and the smaller one for the older. There had been a time in her younger years when Melody had been sweet on Josiah, Jake and Mina's oldest son. It soon became evident that Josiah wasn't interested in a blind girl for a sweetheart, and ever since Melody had come to realize that marriage was not for her. She hoped that someday she would claim the little house for herself. That way she could be independent of her parents but still live close enough to have help when she needed it, which she reluctantly admitted she sometimes did.

Melody's face never changed expression but inwardly she trembled as she thought of her younger sister not being with her day by day this coming winter. As desperately as she tried to be independent, she relied on Harmony in so many ways. How would she ever get along without her? At the same time, she knew it would be a good test of her ability to be independent.

"That was the same fellow that was following you, Melody."

Jasper's voice behind her broke into her thoughts and it took her a moment to understand what he said.

"Not that he was really following you, like I said before, but it's odd that he took off the way he did. Wonder why Pastor Jake went after him." Jasper chuckled. "Guess that's one way to try to save a lost soul."

The others laughed with him, but Melody was silent. She was thinking about the conversation she and Harmony had the night before when Harmony told her about meeting Garrett Foxe in the mercantile. Her sister's voice held a different tone in it than anything Melody had heard there before while she described the man's good looks to her. Melody knew Harmony was a bit of a flirt with her boyhood friends. It worried her a little that her sister seemed taken by this new man.

Jasper spoke quietly just for her to hear him. "Nothing to worry about, Mel. I think Pastor Jake thought the fellow was someone he knew and he just wanted to speak to him."

"If you ask me," Melody heard Eve's voice on her right. "I think Dad looked like he'd seen a ghost!"

"You and your imagination!" Naomi chided her sister.

Jasper patted Melody's arm. "Well, who would like a ride home? Looks like your folks are going to be talking for a while yet."

"I'll go with you." Harmony spoke quickly.

Melody heard some of the others agree as well.

"You coming, Melody?"

She shook her head. "No thanks, I'll wait for my mom and dad."

"I'm riding with Torkel, Melody." Eve squeezed Melody's hand. "See you later, okay?"

"Okay." *"See you later."* Melody smiled to herself. So many expressions used sight terms. She and Harmony and Eve often laughed at how funny they sounded to a blind person. She sighed quietly.

"Wanna climb in, Mel?"

Melody took Tobias's hand as he helped her into the surrey. At fourteen he was the youngest of her brothers and shared a special relationship with her. She had helped care for all her younger siblings as babies but had spent the most time caring for Tobias when her mother was busy with the needs of the rest of her growing family. It had been her privilege to help in their schooling as well as she worked with Miss Emerson, the teacher in their one-room school.

"Something troubling you, Mel?"

She turned to him. "Why do you ask?"

"You sighed."

Melody smiled. Of course Tobias would notice that. "I was just thinking how happy I am for Harmony to get that teaching job and how lonely it will be without her around the house. And I guess I'm a little sad that Torkel won't be living in the same house even though he'll be close by."

"That's what I figured. You've still got me! I'm never leaving to get married."

"Oh, Toby!" Melody laughed. "One day I'll remind you that you said that."

"Nope. Not me. Maybe you'll get married."

Melody shook her head. "No. If you're not, then I'll just have to stay around and take care of you."

"But maybe you will get married, Mel. You're awfully pretty, you know. I see fellers look at you all the time."

Melody patted Tobias on the arm. "Uh huh. They're looking and wondering why I keep bumping into things." She shook her head again. "No, Toby. No one wants to take care of a blind wife."

"I bet Josiah or Jasper would marry you."

"Jasper! Good grief, Toby! He's like a brother or an uncle, not a husband! You get that idea out of your head right now, and for goodness' sake, don't ever say anything like that to him! And…and just forget about Josiah too, okay?"

"Okay, okay. Didn't mean to rile you up. Here come Mom and Dad."

Melody felt the surrey sway as her father helped her mother onto the front seat and climbed on after her.

"Where are the others?" Her mother asked.

"They all rode with Jasper." Tobias explained. "Torkel took Eve with him."

"Of course." Melody knew her mother was smiling.

"Did Jake say why he cut the service short?" Melody asked her father. She waited for an answer and wondered why he delayed.

"Guess he had his reasons. At least we got out early for once." He chuckled.

There's something he's not saying. Melody supposed that they didn't want to discuss what was going on in front of Tobias and hoped they would tell her what they knew later. At nineteen, her parents treated her as an adult, and she appreciated that. She also knew that since she would never marry, she would most likely be dependent on them for the rest of her life. That was another thing she wanted to discuss with them when they had a private moment.

Sunday dinner was always a special occasion and even more so today when Melody learned that the Rodwells had decided to join them. Mina sent her children home to bring the food she had prepared to pair up with the food that the Wheatlys had ready. It was a noisy gathering, and Melody delighted in listening to all the conversations going on from the dining room table to the living room where a table had been set up for the younger children. As all were now at least in their teens, the growing families needed more room to spread out.

"Your crops look good this year, Keane. Tuva, this corn-on-the-cob is the sweetest yet." Jake was saying.

Melody left the dining room to bring a refilled bowl of potatoes to the living room.

"Tobias, you've got butter all down your chin! Use a napkin!" Harmony scolded her brother.

"Quit bossing me around or I'll tell Ma about you making eyes at Jasper." Tobias retorted.

Melody stopped short with the bowl in her hands.

"Here, I'll take that, Melody."

She passed the bowl to Naomi and turned back to the other room. She could hear Harmony whisper to Tobias, "You do and I'll—"

"Everything going okay in there, Melody? Do they need anything else?" Her mother asked Melody as she returned to her seat with the adults.

"Sounded like they were doing just fine unless Toby needs more napkins for the butter on his chin."

The others laughed.

"You just can't help but get messy eating corn this way, and there's nothing better!" Her dad proclaimed.

They finished the meal and the cleanup in record time with all hands pitching in. Melody knew the house and kitchen so well that she moved among the people without any mishaps. The unspoken rule of the house was to not change the location of things. Every plate, cup, glass, or piece of silverware went back in the exact same spot it came from so that Melody could find it. Years of working side-by-side with her mother had enabled her to be able to cook a meal with ease.

Melody took down cups for the coffee that was brewing. Eve and Torkel had gone for a walk, and the boys were outside getting ready for a game of baseball. Naomi, at fifteen, felt she was too old for the boys' game and had decided to walk home, and Harmony excused herself to do some studying, so that left Mina and Jake in the living room with her parents. Melody wondered if they wanted privacy or if she would be welcome to join them.

The aroma of the coffee was enticing. Melody sliced into the blueberry pies she and her mother had baked the day before and began sliding the pieces onto plates. The grownups would have their dessert first, and the boys would be in later for theirs. She picked up the coffee pot and began pouring the hot liquid into the cups, placing her finger a little inside the rim until the liquid reached its level. She placed four cups on the tray first and carried them into the next room.

"Oh, I should be out there helping you, Melody. I'm sorry." Her mother took the tray from her.

"No problem. I have the pie ready too. Be back in a moment."

"There are only four cups here. Why don't you join us, dear?"

Melody nodded her agreement and went back for the dessert. When she was seated with her coffee beside her and her pie in front of her, she waited for the conversation to continue.

Jake spoke first. "Melody, I was telling your parents that the reason I ran out of church was because the fellow I spotted in the back row looked just like Mina's brother Thorpe. Now, we know it couldn't be him because he died over twenty years ago, but I have to say it shook me up some to see this man who looked so much like him. Harmony met him at the mercantile and said his name is Garrett Foxe."

"He has to be a relative, Jake. I mean, he could be my nephew or something." Mina added. "And if he is, my parents need to know."

"Keane, I assume you've told Melody our whole story." Jake spoke again.

Her father cleared his throat, and Melody heard him sip at his coffee. "All our children have heard the entire tale even the part about me running away from God."

Melody nodded but kept quiet.

"Jasper said this was the man who followed you back from the cemetery, Melody. Can you tell us anything about that?"

Melody heard something in her father's voice that set her heart to beating a bit faster. He was worried.

"I knew someone else was there because of the birds." She shrugged. "You know what I mean."

"Yes, dear. We know you sense things stronger than the rest of us because of your blindness. I have always been thankful for that." Her mother responded.

"Well, I knew it wasn't someone from town because they would have spoken to me, so it made me nervous and I just left. I could hear him behind me, but I wasn't really afraid of him. He kept back."

Keane spoke again. "I want you to be careful, Mel. We don't know who this Garrett Foxe is or if he even is related to Thorpe, but if he is, we need to find out what he wants here. It could be he's after revenge for what happened to Thorpe."

"Revenge? It was Thorpe who caused all the trouble in the first place!" Melody didn't understand.

"Well, Garrett was at the cemetery. That means he was looking at a grave, and that grave could be Thorpe's. Now, we may be jumping to conclusions, but I think we need to be on our guard. He may know only part of the story and not know how things ended here when Thorpe died. We need some answers, so until we know more, I don't want you walking about on your own, Melody."

Melody took a deep breath. "Okay, Dad. But...will you and Jake be okay?"

She felt her father's arm go around her shoulders and she leaned into him. "Don't worry about us, sweetheart. We'll get the answers and put everyone's minds at ease. I'll talk to the other kids too. The only way to keep safe is to keep informed. I don't want there to be secrets."

"Let's give it to the Lord, shall we?"

Melody bowed her head with the others as Jake led in prayer. She felt her mother take hold of her hand.

They're mostly worried about me because I'm the most vulnerable. They will always be worried about me.

It was routine at bedtime that Melody would recall events of the day and ask Harmony to describe to her the things she had not been able to see for herself. She first asked about Jake racing down the aisle at church. She had heard the commotion, but needed to get a picture of it in her mind to better understand it.

This had become a tradition for the girls. Harmony was Melody's eyes in so many ways. When Melody caught the fragrance of a blossom, Harmony brought it to her and described it as Melody lightly ran her fingers over it. Though she didn't know color, she knew the color names and could associate a color with another item that had been described to her. Once Harmony told her that her eyes were the same icy blue as their mother's, as blue as a frozen lake. Having no clue exactly what that meant, she still found comfort in knowing she resembled her mother in some way.

Next she asked Harmony about the man who ran from the church. "Are you sure he was the same man you met in the mercantile? You heard Dad say that he looks like Thorpe Prescott."

She felt Harmony's hesitation. "It's odd, Mel. Garrett Foxe is quite handsome really, with dark hair and eyes. He does resemble Mina a bit, and when I first saw him, I thought right away that he looked how Mr. Prescott, Mina's dad, must have looked when he was young. But…"

"What?"

"I guess I keep thinking how evil Thorpe was to Dad and Jake, but I didn't see that in Garrett. He was quite pleasant, actually."

Melody heard that tone in her sister's voice again.

The girls were silent, each in their own thoughts. Then Melody spoke. "Were you making eyes at Jasper?"

"Oh, Mel! You know me better than that. Jasper's old! I just figured that if I showed some interest in him, it might make Josiah take notice."

"Josiah?"

Harmony yawned and rolled over. "At least it made Josiah more aware of me."

Melody was stunned at her sister's words. "Since when have you been interested in Josiah?"

There was no answer, but Melody persisted. "Harmony, it's not right to use Jasper to make Josiah jealous. You could hurt Jasper."

Harmony's words were muffled. "Jasper wouldn't care."

Yes he would. Melody knew Jasper better than her sister did. Jasper spent a lot of time with the Wheatly family, and Melody was pretty sure it was partly because of her vivacious sister. She knew Harmony attracted the attention of the male population in the area, and Jasper would be no exception. He had always been good to Melody and she didn't want to see him get hurt. If he truly were interested in Harmony, then she was going to make sure her sister respected that.

Harmony and Josiah. It stung a little to know that Josiah could very well become sweet on Harmony. Melody well remembered a few years back when she had walked home from school with the others and she and Josiah had fallen behind. She had been thrilled to have some time alone with him, hoping he reciprocated her feelings, but that thought had soon been dashed when Josiah had flatly stated that no doubt her parents would be taking care of her the rest of her life. He meant no harm, but his words hit her like a physical blow. Somewhere in her adolescent thinking she had dreams of a husband and her own home one day. Those dreams were taken away from her in that moment, and the reality and harshness of life had taken over. She was actually thankful for Josiah setting her straight. And even though she knew Josiah would find and marry someone someday and that it would hurt her when he did, she never thought she would have to deal with it being her own sister.

After Harmony fell asleep beside her, Melody turned her thoughts back to the story her father and mother had told of their encounter with Thorpe Prescott.

Keane Wheatly and Jake Rodwell had been shanghaied and were on a ship with Thorpe as the first mate. Thorpe was a cruel master, torturing the captured seamen into submission, even killing those who disobeyed. It was Jake's plan and a violent storm that helped the two men escape by God's grace, though barely with their lives. They made their way back from the west coast to Keane's parents' farm in Minnesota, and along the way Jake led Keane, her father, to the Lord. Life was going well for the two men until one day Thorpe and his minions came for their revenge and nearly killed them and her Grandpa Wheatly. Mina and Tuva were there in the barn when Thorpe, not knowing that Mina was his own sister, whipped her in order to get the men to do his bidding. Grandma Wheatly and another couple stopped them, and Thorpe was shot. Just before he died, Jake told Thorpe that his sins could be forgiven if he trusted in Christ's sacrifice for them on the cross. In those final moments before he drew his last breath, Thorpe believed.

Melody felt a tear slip out of her eye toward the pillow as she recalled her father's admission of what he did next. He was so angry that Thorpe, who deserved to die and deserved to go to hell, would instead be welcomed into heaven, that he fled the farm and tried to flee from God. He wanted nothing to do with a God who would save a man like Thorpe. But through the prayers of his loved ones and the testimony of a man who worked with him in the lumber camp, he realized that God's grace was more than *he* deserved as well.

What if this Garrett Foxe is Thorpe's son? What did he want here in Ulen? Was he after revenge?

three

Garrett stood again in the cemetery in front of the gravestone, staring down at it as if the answers to his questions could be found there.

Maybe I shouldn't have come here.

That preacher had looked at Garrett as if he were afraid of him.

I must look like this Thorpe Prescott. What did Thorpe do to make someone afraid of him?

He headed back to town, wondering what his next step should be. He was here to find out more about this man whose name was on that grave. He had only just learned of Thorpe's existence when his mother died and he went through her things. The papers he found had astounded him.

Garrett needed to talk to that preacher. That man knew something. And whether it was good news or bad news, as he feared, he needed to know. But working at the mercantile wouldn't enable him the freedom to seek the preacher out. He was about to ask Ole for a day off when the storekeeper announced that he wasn't needed the following day because his wife came in every Tuesday to clean the store.

"She doesn't even like *me* being in the way, so it's best if you aren't either." The man told him with an apologetic grin. "See you on Wednesday."

"Yes, sir. I was wondering if you could tell me where that preacher lives, the one from the church down the road."

"You mean Jake Rodwell? You just follow the road there east out of town…"

Garrett tapped the reins on the back of the horse as he made his way past the buildings in town out to the open prairie. The buggy swayed a bit as a horseless carriage made its way past him, and the horse side-stepped when the driver honked his horn. Garrett was used to the new automobiles, but he was surprised to see this one, the first he had seen since being in Ulen. It somehow seemed out of place in this quiet town. Horses and oxen were still plentiful, but it seemed progress was finding its way even here.

The prairie was new to him too. He could see no end to it, and its vastness awed him. Here and there he could make out various crops growing in the fields. He didn't know much about farming, but he found it all so interesting. He breathed deeply, amazed at the freshness of the air. No coal soot or garbage or fishy smell to contend with here. He wrinkled his nose. Although there was an occasional whiff of manure.

As he got closer to his destination, he could see men out in the fields. It was the beginning of harvest time and they seemed busy at their work. He wondered if the man he was coming to see was among them. Surely a preacher wouldn't be working on a farm, would he?

He debated how he was going to explain his rapid departure from the church. The fact that the preacher's shocked face had scared him into running away hardly seemed like a plausible explanation, yet that was the truth. Maybe he should start with asking the man why he had stared at him in such a manner. Maybe that would answer his questions.

A farmhouse was up ahead and Garrett slowed the horse and then stopped altogether. He recognized the young woman in the garden as the girl from the cemetery, the one Harmony Wheatly called Melody. She had just stood up to stretch and was again kneeling down and appeared to be picking something and putting it into a basket. He urged the horse a little closer and stopped again to watch her.

She seemed unaware of his presence. He noticed the buildings were well kept: a farmhouse, a smaller house, a barn, a corral, and a chicken coop. Melody was apparently done with her picking as she stood and started back toward the house. On the way, she set the basket down and reached for something hanging from a tree. Garrett peered closer to see what she was doing. It was some kind of sack on a rope. She held it with one hand as she climbed the tree it was attached to and then jumped onto the sack and swung. Her dress and her hair flew back and forth with each swing. It looked like such fun that Garrett found himself smiling.

When the swing stopped, the girl got off and walked back to where she had left her basket. For a few moments she felt along the ground until she came upon the handle. Then she picked it up and straightened her skirt and headed to the doorway of the house.

Garrett stared after her, his mouth going dry. Though she was some distance away, he could see her quite clearly. He could see her mussed blonde hair, he could see the color in her cheeks, he could see the smile on her face expressing joy in her childlike abandonment on the swing.

And he could see her sightless eyes.

He could see.

She could not.

He closed his eyes remembering her at the cemetery and how she had felt the headstone and traced the words. He remembered how she called out for Harmony, who came and took her by the arm. He remembered her playing the piano without the help of a music book.

He felt sick. He didn't know why. He didn't know this girl, but she was young and lovely and to see her feeling about for that basket made him feel sorry for her, sorry for her blindness.

He heard someone call out and he looked up. A couple of men from the field were making their way toward him, but for some reason he again felt he had to get away. He couldn't talk now, not feeling the way he did. Turning the buggy, he slapped the reins and let the horse move swiftly away from the farmhouse.

"Dad! Wasn't that the man from the church?" Torkel called out the question as he and Aslak and Tobias followed their father.

Keane turned to Jake who ran up to him. "It was him again, Jake. I don't like this. He was watching the house. I better go check on the women."

Jake shaded his eyes to see the retreating buggy. "It's okay, boys." He nodded to his own sons, Josiah and Aaron, who joined them. "I think it's time we have a talk with this Garrett Foxe. Until we get answers I want one of you at each house, keeping an eye on things. Josiah, you take first watch at our place. Torkel, check in with your dad and tell him what I said. The rest of us will finish up in this field then Keane and I will take a ride into town."

The boys sent anxious looks over their shoulders as they headed out to do their work.

Keane and Jake were quiet as they rode into town. They had talked things out with their wives and families before cleaning up and starting out with instructions to their eldest sons to be on guard. It was Keane who broke the silence first.

"I thought that nightmare was over."

Jake glanced at him, noting his tight jaw and stern expression, then looked away. "It is over. I think we're on edge just because we don't know what to expect. And that's good. We need to be prepared for anything, but we have to keep in mind that it all may be nothing more than some stranger looking to buy land or something just as innocent."

"He was watching the house." Keane held Jake's gaze. "Tuva saw him just as Melody came in from picking beans. He just sat there staring at the house, Jake."

"Okay. So, we'll ask him what he was doing there and what he wants and then we'll know."

"Suppose we should get the sheriff to come along?"

Jake shifted on the buggy seat. "Oh, I don't think we have to involve the sheriff at this point. We'll go to the hotel and ask to have him meet us in the lobby. It will be better if other people are around."

The two men arrived in town just as the train was coming in. They paid it no mind as they headed to the Orient Hotel. The man behind the counter was slumped in his chair with his feet crossed on the desk in front of him. A slight snore rumbled from his chest with every breath. Jake grinned at Keane before he tapped the bell on the counter, sending the man into an upright position as his feet hit the floor.

"Hello. What? Welcome to the Orient—" He blinked his eyes at the two men who stood grinning on the other side of the counter. "Why you—what's the idea waking a hard-working man?"

Keane laughed out loud and Jake reached across the counter and slapped the man on the shoulder. "Sorry to wake you, Knute. Would you mind getting that new guy for us? Garrett Foxe? Ask him to come down to the lobby."

The man named Knute rubbed at his eyes. "Can't you go get him yerself? Them stairs are a killer."

"I know, Knute. Please?"

"Oh, all right."

Jake headed to the lobby and Keane followed, watching as Knute made his slow way up the staircase. "I feel kind of bad making old Knute go after him."

"Better than us doing it. Sit down a minute. I've been thinking. Let's just welcome the guy and let him do the explaining. We'll know if he's hedging about and not telling the truth. If that's the case, we can go ahead and ask our questions, but let's give him a chance first. Okay?"

Keane nodded. They both looked up as they heard footsteps on the stairs. The young man hesitated when he saw the two men waiting for him, but he continued descending with Knute lumbering behind him.

The resemblance to Thorpe struck Jake again as he held out his hand and struggled to put a smile on his face. There was still no way to know if he was facing a friend or foe. "Hello. I'm Jake Rodwell and this is Keane Wheatly. Welcome to Ulen."

The man shook hands with both of them but was obviously uncomfortable. "Thank you. I'm Garrett. Garrett Foxe." He fumbled with straightening his jacket. "Look, I'm sorry about running out of your church yesterday."

Jake motioned for them to sit down. He glanced briefly at Keane as if to gauge his reaction. "Oh, that's all right. It's not the first time someone has gotten up and left in the middle of one of my sermons." He chuckled to ease the man's obvious tension. "Sometimes they even fall asleep."

Garrett smiled slightly.

Jake decided to get right to the point. "I think I might know why you left. I was startled and I stared at you when I saw you because you remind me so much of someone I used to know." He let that statement sink in and was rewarded with a stunned expression on the young man's face.

"Who do I remind you of?"

Jake never took his gaze off Garrett. "His name was Thorpe Prescott. Did you know him?"

It was obvious that the name meant something to Garrett. He leaned forward with interest, but he shook his head. "No, no I didn't know him."

Jake let out the breath he had been holding. Keane inched forward on his chair. "But the name means something to you, Mr. Foxe, doesn't it? You look so much like him."

Garrett searched the men's faces, looking from one to the other. "Will you tell me about him?"

Jake glanced at Keane again. "First, what is it you want to know? And why do you want to know?"

Garrett looked at the floor. In almost a whisper, he answered, "I believe he was my father."

Silence.

"You believe?"

Garrett nodded. "After my mother died, I found some papers. There was a marriage certificate with her name and his name on it, and my birth certificate with his name as my father."

Keane frowned. "But...you didn't know this until...when?"

"My mother died two months ago."

"She never told you?"

Garrett took a deep breath. "She told me that my father was a sailor and that he drowned in a shipwreck. She said his name was Gavin Foxe." He didn't look up. "I don't know why she lied. She was a good mother and worked hard to provide for me, but we had many struggles. We stayed in Seattle until I was ten then all of a sudden we packed up and headed to Chicago where my mother had an old school friend that I never knew of either. We stopped here in Ulen on the way and went to the cemetery. I guess she wanted proof that he was really dead. I went there a few days ago when I arrived just to make sure myself."

"So that's why you were at the cemetery when my daughter was there." Keane spoke.

"Your daughter, sir?"

"Melody is my oldest. She said she knew someone was there, but when you didn't speak to her, she was afraid. You see, she's blind and the townsfolk would have spoken to let her know they were there."

"I'm sorry I frightened her. I was hoping to talk with her and see if she could answer some of my questions." Garrett turned to Jake again. "I drove out to see you yesterday for the same reason, but then I got scared when you all started coming toward me. There has to be something about this man, this Thorpe Prescott, whom I look like, that scares people. I've told you why I need to know about him. Will you tell me what you know?"

Jake studied the face before him. Garrett looked so much like Thorpe that it was uncanny and a bit unnerving as well. But Jake could hear the sincerity in the man's voice and knew he had to tell him the truth.

"First of all, let me assure you that your father made a decision before he died to accept the Lord Jesus Christ as his Savior. He placed his faith in the death, burial, and resurrection of the Lord Jesus for his sins. He is now in heaven and if you know the Lord, you will see him there."

Garrett listened with interest, his face lighting up. "So, he was a good man?"

Keane stood abruptly and walked to the window. Garrett watched him, puzzlement on his face before giving Jake his attention again.

"No, Mr. Foxe, he was not a good man." The words were spoken as an apology.

Garrett frowned. "But you said…you said he's in heaven."

"Yes, I did, and he is. In his dying breath he believed and was saved. It only takes a moment to place your faith in Christ, and Thorpe knew he wasn't good enough to get to heaven on his own merits. He knew he was a sinner and needed a Savior, and he made the right decision to accept the work Jesus did for him. None of us get to heaven by being good because we can't be good enough."

Jake would have continued but he could see that the young man was not focused on what he was saying. He waited and saw Garrett frown.

"Okay. In his dying breath he made a decision and now he's in heaven." Garrett looked over to Keane who had turned back to watch him. "What about before that? What was he like before he made his deathbed decision?"

Jake sighed. "I'm sorry to have to tell you this."

Garrett stared at the ceiling in his room, watching the moonlight dance through the curtains onto the walls.

He believed everything the men said.

So now he knew. His father was a kidnapper, a brutal man, even a murderer. No wonder his mother made up a fictitious man for her son. She never wanted him to know what a monster his real father was. Thorpe had the two men shanghaied, he tortured them, he nearly killed them, and when they escaped from him, he went after them and tried to kill not only them but Keane's father as well. He even brutalized his own sister.

But he must have been different at one time or else why would she have married him? She was a good mother and did her best to raise him right. Why would a man like the one Mr. Rodwell and Mr. Wheatly described have been attracted to a good, simple woman like his mother? What caused them to separate? Why did his mother stay in Seattle until she had word that he was dead? Why did she stop in this prairie town to see the grave for herself?

Garrett rolled over to his side. So many questions still. He thought if he could at least learn a bit about the man in that cemetery, he would be satisfied, but he was not. Would he ever be?

That business about Thorpe being in heaven now, Garrett dismissed that. That was preacher talk, nothing more. A man like Thorpe Prescott had no right to heaven. Jake Rodwell was just doing his job trying to comfort him.

Garrett got up and went to the window. It was a cooler night and the moonlight was spectacular. He leaned out the window and listened to the chirps of the crickets and grasshoppers. He straightened up and leaned his arm against the pane. They offered him a job and a place to stay, saying he was *family* after all.

He had an aunt! And grandparents! And cousins!

After his mother's friend passed away, it was just the two of them again, he and his mother. They had to move out of her old friend's house into a small apartment in a terrible neighborhood. He left soon after his mother's death, choosing to come to Ulen to find out about the man he learned was his father. Now to find that he had actual relatives was a shock. He was to meet them all tomorrow. They wanted him to stay with them. It would be a little crowded at first, they said, but Eve would be moving out soon to marry Keane's son Torkel.

He told the men he would meet with them, but he wasn't ready to make a decision on staying here. At twenty-five he should be established, have a home, a wife, a family, yet his had not been a normal life. Now he was running out of money, so where else would he go?

four

Chicago

The law office of Wilson & Krause had barely opened when a young man pushed open the door and rushed to the office of its senior partner.

"Mr. Wilson, I just got news that Gordon Fairfax died last night."

Behind the large oak desk a man, graying at the temples, leaned back in his leather chair. "You're sure about this?"

"Yes, sir. I went by the place this morning to verify it, and then I came straight here."

"Good work, Bill. Send in my secretary, would you, please?"

The young man nodded and hurried out to do his boss's bidding. This was big news and a thrill of excitement ran through the man. He straightened his tie and sat down at his desk, a smaller version of the one owned by the senior partners, but impressive enough. He was an apprentice, still learning the trade, but often treated like an errand boy. He waited, knowing what task his boss was going to ask of him next.

"Mr. Gladstone, Mr. Wilson would like to see you."

Bill gave the secretary a saucy wink and headed to the main office. He knocked sharply on the door and entered when given permission.

"You wanted me, sir?"

Mr. Wilson was folding a note into an envelope before he handed it over to Bill. There were papers neatly piled about the man's desk and an unopened packet sat in front of him. "Get this to the Merchants' Savings, Loan, and Trust Co. and tell them to send their chief officer over."

"Yes, sir. Right away."

Bill contained his excitement until he was out of the building. Getting the job at Wilson & Krause had been no easy feat, but once there he worked hard to earn the trust of his employers. The envelope in his hand might just be the break he had been hoping for, and as soon as he was out of sight of the building, he stopped and carefully opened the seal on the envelope. Reading the missive brought a frown to his face. Who was Garrett Foxe Prescott?

Ulen

"He's our cousin?"

"You asked him to live with us?"

"What did he say? Have you told Grandpa and Grandma?"

Jake shook his head at his children and their questions. He had spent most of the night talking with Mina about Garrett Foxe and had just announced the news to the rest of the family when the inquisition started.

"What was he doing watching Wheatly's house?" Josiah asked. "Are you sure we can trust him?"

Jake saw his son's concern. "He said he was on his way to talk to me and then got scared when we all started coming toward him."

"Scared of what? It still doesn't explain why he sat there so long."

"Let's give him the benefit of the doubt, son. Remember, he's just learned who his father was and the kind of man he was. It's a lot to take in and he's probably feeling uncomfortable about the whole thing himself. As far as I can tell, we're the only family he has now that his mother has died. And from his reaction to what I told him about his father getting saved, I don't believe he knows the Lord. Keep that in mind. You four have an opportunity to share Christ's love for him with him."

"Do you like him, Pa?"

Jake smiled at his youngest daughter. At fifteen she was between being a young lady and an awkward adolescent, and it was hard as a father to see the little girl no longer there. "I do, Naomi. He's had a hard time of it and he needs us."

"Okay, Pa. Let's go get him."

Josiah and Aaron rode horseback while the others rode in the wagon. Mina requested that she be dropped off at her parents' house to prepare them before Jake and the children brought Garrett there. It was going to be a shock, but she and Jake knew they would gladly welcome this unexpected grandchild into their lives.

Garrett was waiting in front of the hotel when they arrived. The boys swung down from their horses, and Jake helped Eve and Naomi step from the wagon. Garrett stood, but it was Jake who made the first move.

"Let me introduce you to your cousins, Garrett. Oldest at twenty-one, our son Josiah."

Josiah held out his hand. "Good to know you, Garrett."

"This is our next in line, Eve. She and Keane's oldest son Torkel will be married soon." Eve stepped forward and shook hands with Garrett. "Then we have Aaron, he's seventeen, and here's the baby, Naomi."

"Oh, Pa! You can't keep calling me the baby when I'm already fifteen. Hi Garrett. Welcome to the family."

Garrett finished shaking hands with the four young people. He seemed a bit uneasy. "I've never had cousins. Do I call you Miss Rodwell or Cousin Naomi?"

Naomi laughed then realized he was serious. "You can call me whatever you like, Garrett, but I'd prefer Naomi."

"I think she'd prefer *Your Highness.*" Aaron teased.

Naomi elbowed her brother and stepped closer to Garrett and took his arm. "Pay him no mind. Come on. We're going to take you to meet Grandpa and Grandma. You are going to love them!"

Garrett allowed the girl to lead him to the wagon while Josiah picked up his bag and tossed it in the back, giving a nod to Garrett when he thanked him. Jake was inwardly relieved at the way things were going so far. He had feared Garrett might have high-tailed it out of town after what he and Keane had relayed to him about his father, but the young man was still here. *"I pray, Lord, that we can show him your love and that he'll accept your gift of salvation."* There was still much that they didn't know about Garrett Foxe, but hopefully over time Garrett would open up to them.

The Prescotts lived in a gray house not far from the main street of Ulen. The small front yard was neatly trimmed, and Garrett immediately noticed a birdhouse, a miniature replica of the house, on a pole near the street. Huge white hydrangea blossoms met them on either side of the door as Garrett let the Rodwell family lead him up the path to be welcomed by a pretty woman with dark hair, who looked very much like the girls Eve and Naomi. She stood holding her hand over her mouth as she stared at Garrett, and he could see tears glistening in her eyes. Her children stepped back, away from Garrett as their mother slowly approached him. He was uncertain of what to do as no one said anything, so he started to hold out his hand to introduce himself when with a rush the woman ran to him and flung her arms around him.

Garrett felt the *oomph* of the impact move him back a step and was surprised that such a small woman could almost knock him over. He looked over the woman's head to see that Eve and Naomi were wiping away tears and laughing at the same time. Jake came to his rescue.

"Meet my wife, your Aunt Mina, Garrett. She is your father's sister."

Mina stepped back but kept her arms locked around Garrett. She looked up at him and smiled through her tears. "I am so, so happy that you're here, Garrett! Oh, my goodness!" She squeezed him again. "I have a nephew!" She released her hold, much to Garrett's relief as he drew in a needed breath, noting that as he did so Josiah and Aaron grinned at him. The friendliness this family was showing him melted away some of the uneasiness that had built up in him overnight as he pondered the things Keane and Jake had told him about Thorpe Prescott. By all rights, they should have hatred toward the man who tried to kill them and who had hurt them all, and logically, to him anyway, that hatred should spread to him. Why, this woman who was grasping his arm even now and chattering on about meeting his grandparents, she was whipped by the man who was his father! How could she welcome the son of such a man into her home?

They were at the door now and Garrett tried to concentrate on the woman's words, which had been coming out of her mouth in a steady stream.

"They were as shocked as the rest of us to learn that Thorpe had a son, but let me assure you, Garrett, that they are excited to meet you and to get to know you. Right off, they wanted you to stay here in town with them, but Jake and I talked and we really want you to be a part of the family out at the farm. Of course, the decision is yours, but we really, really want you, and Grandpa and Grandma come out all the time so you'll get to see them as much as we do and—"

"Okay, Mina, he gets the idea. Take a breath and let Garrett in the house."

Mina blushed as she squeezed Garrett's arm again. "I'm just so happy to see you! I don't want to let go of you!"

Jake was laughing as he took his wife's other arm and gently pulled her back so that Garrett could step up to the doorway. Garrett smiled at Mina and back at the others who were laughing at their mother's enthusiasm. He looked up just as the screen door opened and an older couple stepped out. They had been at the door, watching their daughter's actions and they were smiling with the others.

Garrett's smile froze on his face. The older, white-haired woman was small like Mina, and was now staring at him with tears freely rolling down her cheeks, but it was the man who had Garrett's attention. Looking at him was like seeing an older version of himself. There was a slight stoop to the man's shoulders and his eyes behind the spectacles he wore were not as bright as they must have once been, but the resemblance was still there. This was his grandfather.

The woman opened her arms and Garrett stepped into her embrace. He felt her tremble as she whispered, "You look just like your grandpa when I married him."

He smiled down at her. "Yes, I believe I see some resemblance."

Looking at the older man, he held out his hand. "Garrett Foxe, sir. I believe I am your grandson."

Mr. Prescott took the hand and pulled Garrett into an embrace. "I believe you're right. Welcome home, Garrett. We're Grandpa and Grandma to you. Come in, come in everyone! Grandma has tea and lemonade and cookies all ready, and we have a lot to talk about."

The visit went by in a blur to Garrett. These people were his family, his relatives. He had so much to take in and they were sharing stories so quickly that he was having trouble grasping it all. The Prescotts brought out some pictures they had, though not many, of their son Thorpe. The childhood pictures helped tell the story of his father's life, but the story ended when he was sixteen and left home. After that, the family knew nothing of him until his visit to Ulen to seek revenge on Keane and Jake. In fact, even then his grandparents never saw their son alive again.

"What I can't understand is why Keane and I never saw Thorpe's resemblance to Grandpa Prescott that is so obvious now when we see Garrett." Jake frowned. "The only reason I can think of is that Thorpe's expression was always dark and wicked, so different from yours, Garrett. But I knew right away when I saw you in church that you looked like Thorpe, and Keane said the same thing when he saw you in the mercantile."

Garrett thought a minute. "Maybe I was scowling those times."

Jake laughed. "And Grandpa never scowls, so there's no comparison."

"I do too!" Grandpa Prescott contorted his face into his fiercest frown, making them all laugh.

Garrett had never enjoyed himself so much.

They had questions for Garrett too that he found difficult to answer. He could tell them nothing of why his mother lied about his father's identity because he didn't know the answers himself. He told them a little about the hardships he and his mother endured, trying to survive on their own, but he refrained from revealing too much. He didn't want their sympathy, and the past was the past. He wanted to move on.

"I'm not sure what to do now." He admitted. "I came here to find out about my father, and now that I've done that, I'm not sure where to go from here."

"We'd like you to stay." Mina spoke up from her place beside Garrett on the sofa. She slipped her arm around him. "Please!"

Garrett smiled shyly at his aunt. He liked Mina. He liked them all. "I can't just stay with you. I need to earn some money. I was working at the mercantile—"

"You can work with us," Aaron spoke up. "Eve's getting married next month, and I don't mind sharing the chores with you."

"Aaron!"

Aaron grinned at his father's reprimand, making the others laugh. Garrett joined in.

"I'd like to help out. I guess if you're all okay with me staying a while, I'll try to pull my weight."

"Of course we want you to stay. Well, that's settled. We better get home then. Thank you, Mom and Dad, for the refreshments and don't forget, we want you to come for Sunday dinner. We still have a lot of catching up to do with Garrett." Mina hugged her parents. Garrett watched as the others lined up to hug their grandparents, apparently a common practice. He wasn't sure what to do until Naomi gave him a little shove and he found himself enveloped in his grandmother's embrace again. He hugged his grandfather next and followed the others to the wagon. It was a strange, new feeling to be a part of a group—a family. He felt tears sting his eyes and he blinked rapidly to keep them at bay.

They made a quick stop at the mercantile so Garrett could let Mr. Asleson know that he wouldn't be returning for work. He also explained to the man his newly discovered relationship to the Rodwells.

"That's why you looked familiar!" Ole nodded that he understood. "Well, isn't that something!"

Mina talked most of the way to the farm, pointing out places that might interest him. Eve and Naomi added information to what their mother was saying, and Garrett found that despite his earlier uneasiness, he was beginning to relax. When they came by the Wheatly's farm, Jake slowed the horses.

"We've got chores to take care of at home, but later we'll bring you over and introduce you to the rest of Keane's family."

Garrett nodded that he understood. He kept looking at the Wheatly farm as they drove down the driveway across from it. Then he saw her. She came out the doorway with a basket in her hands and started toward the garden. She lifted her head and waved her hand at the wagon. Garrett jumped when Naomi hollered, "Hi, Melody!" beside him.

"That's Melody." Eve explained. "She's a year older than me, but she's younger than Josiah. We're very close."

"Uh…she's…isn't she blind?" Garrett hesitated.

Eve frowned for a moment. "Oh, that's right! You saw her in town. Yes, she's been blind from birth, but you'd hardly know it. She does most of the things we all do. She even helps teach school."

"But, she waved at us. How did she know?"

"Mel knows what our wagon sounds like." Naomi's explanation was matter-of-fact. "She knows all the neighbors' wagons and buggies and surreys, especially Mr. Stende's when he brings the mail. I think she knows most of the horses too, but I'm not sure how she knows."

Mina turned from the front wagon seat. "God has given Melody a special gift in the way she uses her other senses that help make up for her blindness. She's really amazing! And here we are at home! We'll take you around the house first, Garrett, then I'll let the boys show you the rest of the farm. We want to get you settled in and feeling at home as soon as possible."

The next few hours flew by as Garrett was shown around by each of his cousins. Eve and Naomi joined their mother in giving him the *grand tour* as Naomi called it. It was a fairly big house, bigger than any Garrett had lived in, but simply designed and decorated. He would share a bedroom on the second floor with Aaron and Josiah, and by the way the furniture in the room was crowded together, he understood that they had added the extra bed recently just for him.

The girls had their own rooms also on the second floor. Naomi's was a bit messy with books and drawings scattered about, but Eve's was perfectly neat and very feminine. Jake and Mina's room was on the main floor with the living room and large kitchen and dining room. A separate room held a large desk, and Naomi explained that it was her father's study for preparing his sermons. Until that moment, Garrett had completely forgotten that Jake was a pastor.

Enticing aromas wafted from the stove where Mina was busy stoking up the fire. "Dinner will be ready in about half an hour, so don't let the men keep you out there talking your ear off."

"You, my dear, are the only one who can do that." Jake paused to give Mina a kiss on the cheek before taking Garrett's arm and leading him to the door. "Let's get you out of here before the women have you setting the table."

Garrett was not used to seeing affection and teasing between a husband and wife. He let Jake lead him outside but his mystified expression must have revealed his uncertainty in how to react because Jake laughed. "You'll have to get used to Mina and her chatter. I've never known a woman to talk so much." Then Jake peered closer at Garrett's face. "You're blushing!"

Garrett ducked his head and shrugged his shoulders.

"Ah, I think I see. We're an affectionate family. The hugs, the kiss on the cheek...that's new to you. Is that it?"

Garrett nodded, a bit embarrassed by the admission. "But I think I can get used to it."

The farm was also something new to him. As they walked around, the men explained the outbuildings, the crops, the feed each animal required, the various chores that had to be done to keep the farm operating smoothly. Garrett was fascinated by it all.

"What's that?" He pointed to a machine that looked something like the horseless carriage.

Josiah patted the machine affectionately. "This is a tractor, a Minneapolis Steam Tractor. It is going to replace oxen and horses in the fields, just like the Model T is replacing them on the streets. Farms are modernizing and it's about time. It sure makes the work load easier around here, right, Pa?"

Jake nodded. "But they're expensive, so we better have a good crop, Lord willing, so we can keep up with the payments."

The men worked together on the evening chores, and Garrett found that he was enjoying himself. He was used to hard labor, but all his work had been in cities, whether it was loading barrels of fish as he did in Seattle or working in the meat packing plant in Chicago. There he learned the skills of butchering but fortunately hadn't had to work in the slaughter houses.

Supper was a noisy affair. Between Mina's narrative of the family and Naomi's humorous interjections, Garrett felt completely at ease. The only uncomfortable moment was when the others bowed their heads to pray before the meal. Garrett looked on, wondering what was happening before quickly bowing his head with the others.

Later they walked to the Wheatly farm. The long driveway from the Rodwell farm consisted of two wagon wheel tracks with grass growing between them. From there they crossed the road and were at their neighbor's house. Keane came to the door to greet them.

"Figured you'd be over tonight. Come on in. Tuva and the girls have fresh pies right out of the oven just waiting to be eaten. Aaron, you want to spell Aslak on turning the handle on the ice cream? I think he's getting worn out."

"Sure, Keane!"

The first thing Garrett noticed when he entered the farmhouse was Melody standing by the counter. She was smiling a greeting, but she stayed out of everyone's way as introductions were being made.

"Garrett, this is my wife Tuva. Tuva, meet Mina's nephew Garrett Foxe."

Garrett held his breath as he found himself under scrutiny. Tuva was a beautiful lady and her hair was wrapped around her head in a braid, much like he had seen when she sang at the church. At the moment there was a slight frown on her face and Garrett grew uneasy.

"You look so much like him, yet…there's a difference." She shook her head a little. "Forgive me, Garrett. My mind is in the past."

He slowly let out his breath. "I think I understand, ma'am, after learning something of the past from your husband."

"And we're going to leave the past where it is," Keane declared. "These are our sons, Garrett. This is Torkel, he's twenty and about to become an old married man, and this one is Aslak, he's sixteen, and our youngest is Tobias, and he's fourteen."

Each young man shook hands with the newcomer. Garrett winced a little at the squeeze of his hand from each one of them, but noting their tanned skin and muscular arms, he guessed that they weren't even aware of their own strength.

"This is our daughter Harmony. I think you met her the other day at the mercantile." Harmony smiled and gave Garrett her hand. He was bashful as he took it. Not having much experience with women, he didn't know how to respond to the reaction he had when he held her hand. He dropped it as if stung.

"And over here is our oldest daughter Melody." Keane motioned for Garrett to walk with him to where Melody was standing. She held out her hand, and Garrett reached for it, receiving a firm shake from her.

"Pleased to meet you, Mr. Foxe."

"You as well, Miss Wheatly."

Keane slapped Garrett on the back. "Oh, no need for formality here. You don't mind if he just calls you Melody, do you, Mel?"

"Of course not. Please do."

"And I'm Garrett." Garrett couldn't help smiling at her, even though he realized she wasn't seeing him. There was a moment of awkward silence then Garrett said, "Melody and Harmony are beautiful, musical names." His gaze rested on Harmony again and he was delighted by her blush.

Keane led the way to the living room as Tuva started to explain. "It was Keane's idea—"

"Yes, I take full credit for it. You see, Garrett, my wife has an amazing singing voice like nothing you've ever heard."

"Actually, I did hear her sing, sir, twice in fact, and I agree. It was really amazing."

"You did? Oh yes, at the church. Wait, twice?"

"Yes. Mother and I came through Ulen when I was only ten and we went to the graveyard then. You and your daughters were there and you sang," he said to Tuva.

"You remember that?"

"I remember everything about that day." There was a moment of awkward silence then Garrett broke it by saying, "But your sons' names are quite different."

Keane spoke again. "Well, I wanted to give our children musical names because their mother's music means so much to me. So the girls are Melody and Harmony—"

"And he was going to continue with the boys, but I wouldn't let him." Tuva interrupted.

"Ah, but I did get my way somewhat."

Garrett was enjoying the banter between Keane and Tuva. He looked expectantly at Tuva who was rolling her eyes at her husband.

"We had to compromise. I wanted good Norwegian names for our sons, but Keane was insistent on his names as well, so—"

Keane grinned. "Torkel's second name is Tempo, Aslak's is Alto, and Tobias's is Tenor."

The boys were shaking their heads at their father while the others laughed. Torkel spoke up, his voice filled with longsuffering. "Now that you know, we hope you won't ever mention it to anyone…ever."

Garrett laughed with the others. "So you're Norwegian. I know my mother said we were English, but I don't know about my father." He looked expectantly at Mina.

"We have both English and German on our side," Mina told him. "My name is actually Wilhelmina, which just happened to be Keane's mother's name as well. She went by Helma." She smiled in sympathy at Garrett's expression. "It's all so new to you; you must feel overwhelmed."

"A bit." He admitted. "I thought I'd find answers here, and I have, but it has also brought up new questions that I guess I may never find the answers to, like, why did my mother marry this man? Why did they separate? Why did she lie to me all these years?"

"I'm sorry we can't help you with those answers. Thorpe left when I was still a little girl, so I barely knew him, and he didn't write much to my parents except when he wanted money. We never knew about you and your mother, but if we had, we would have contacted you and tried to get to know you."

Garrett nodded. It was obvious they would have.

"So have you decided what you'll do now?" Keane asked.

Before Garrett could answer, Jake spoke. "He's going to stay with us and help out for now, and he can stay as long as he'd like. We're thankful the Lord has brought him to us, and we're going to do our best to make up for lost time with him."

Garrett nodded. "There's no way I can make up for what my father did to you and your families, but I'd like to apologize—"

Jake cut him off. "*You* owe us no apology, Garrett. We've forgiven Thorpe, and we rejoice that he came to the Lord before he died. You're part of our family now."

Garrett found that he couldn't speak.

Tuva rose. "Melody and I will get some refreshments."

Garrett watched as Melody followed her mother from the room, her movements graceful and sure. He appreciated Tuva taking the attention off him and giving him a chance to recover from his emotions. The kindness of these two families was something he had never experienced. He felt Harmony looking his way, but when he glanced at her, she looked down, the slight blush on her cheeks he again found very becoming.

After the pie and coffee the younger members of the family went out for a quick game of catch, inviting Garrett to join them.

"How about coming for a walk with us instead, Garrett? We'll show you around our farm." Torkel took Eve's hand to help her up.

"I'll come too." Josiah joined in.

"Me too. Come on, Melody." Harmony tapped her sister on the arm.

Garrett rose with the others. To him it seemed that Melody wasn't too keen on the idea, but she followed along, her arm looped into Harmony's.

Torkel and Eve took the lead and explained the outbuildings and crops to Garrett as they walked along. Josiah drifted behind and before long Harmony dropped Melody's arm and slowed her steps to walk with him. That left Melody beside Garrett.

He wasn't sure what to do as Torkel and Eve moved ahead. "Would you like to take my arm?" He asked Melody, his voice a little louder than when he talked with the others.

A slight smile swept over her face then disappeared. "That's not necessary, Garrett. I know our land quite well. But, thank you."

They continued in silence until Torkel and Eve stopped and waited for them. Torkel pointed to a line of young pine trees. "We planted these trees when I was about four years old and they've grown about a foot every year. The soil here is good, really good for our crops."

Garrett nodded toward an opening in the trees. "Where does that path lead?"

"That goes next door to Jasper's house. He lives about a quarter mile from here, but he made the path through the fields because it's quicker than going by road to get here, and it helps Melody get to the schoolhouse, which is on the corner of one of his fields."

"That's right." Garrett turned to Melody. "I understand you help teach school?" Again his voice was slightly raised.

Melody nodded but didn't reply. It was Eve who explained as Harmony came up behind them and again looped her arm with Melody's. Melody heard Josiah's footsteps move away.

"Melody knows all the readers by heart, so she helps the younger kids with their reading and arithmetic while Miss Emerson is busy with the older students. She also plays the piano and helps in so many ways that Miss Emerson said she'd never be able to conduct school without her."

Garrett could see that Melody was embarrassed by her friend's praise. "And, did I hear that you are also a teacher?" he directed the question to Harmony.

"Yes! Uh…I begin next week in Flom, that's a little town…uh…north of here."

Melody felt Harmony move away from her to stand nearer Garrett while she told him about her new job. She was surprised at her sister's stuttering. Harmony had never had trouble talking with anyone before. Was it because she was nervous around Garrett Foxe? Or was she bothered that Josiah had abruptly left her?

Separating herself from the others, Melody walked toward the pines and breathed in their fragrance. She felt relief at not being the center of attention because she felt she was about to burst out in laughter if Garrett *shouted* another question to her. It was common among people who first met her to assume that her hearing was also impaired. She'd had to endure loud conversations until someone came to her rescue. Even now, she could hear Harmony quietly telling Garrett that he didn't need to raise his voice when he spoke to her.

Her family loved her, she knew that. She also knew that her family sheltered and protected her from unpleasant situations and unpleasant people, and she appreciated that, yet, it made her feel like a child. She's not. Lately she's wondered what it would be like to not be surrounded by well-meaning family. Could she handle herself?

A rustle of the pine branches alerted her to a presence. It took only a second for her to know it was Jasper. How she knew was even a mystery to her. She just knew.

"Evening, Jasper."

"Hey, Melody. You got company?"

Melody knew he was looking at Garrett. "Yes, and no. Turns out Garrett Foxe is Mina's nephew, the son of Thorpe Prescott." She let that sink in. Most of the townsfolk knew what had happened on the Wheatly farm over twenty years ago. Jasper had been a boy at the time.

Jasper let out a low whistle. "So...what does he want?" Suspicion tinged the question.

"He wants to know about his father. The Rodwells are accepting him as family and he's going to stay with them."

"Hmm." Melody heard him turn toward her. "I got the paths all cleared for you. I know school starts as soon as harvest is over. It's going to be a busy few weeks coming up."

"Thanks, Jasper. I suppose you can't wait for Miss Emerson to return so you have someone to flirt with."

Jasper's smile was reflected in his voice. "Flirting with schoolteachers is a specialty of mine."

Melody laughed out loud. "Are the men starting on our crops or yours first?"

"We'll start with yours. Mine are smaller, so it won't take too long. I was just on my way over to let your pa know that I'll be here in the morning. You mind giving him that message?"

"Sure. See you in the morning."

"No you won't, but I'll *see* you." Jasper chuckled at his joke and Melody laughed with him. Theirs was an odd friendship. Though eleven years her senior, Jasper had always been a friend to her. Long ago, as a young teenager, when she fought anger and depression because of her blindness, Jasper had been there for her. He helped her through those dark times when her siblings and friends could go off and do things she was unable to do. He seemed to have a special way of caring for a wounded animal, an injured bird, or a suffering girl. He reminded her that God's ways are not our ways, and told her that it wasn't something she had done that caused God to punish her with blindness as she had once thought. It was being born into a sin-cursed world, full of illnesses and debilitating diseases that was the reason. It was a breakthrough for her when she gave her anger over to the Lord and decided to let him use her in whatever condition she was in, and Jasper had helped her do that. She would always be grateful for that.

She wondered why he had never married. Harmony told her that Jasper was good-looking and that the ladies thought him a good catch, what with him having his own farm and all. She had heard him many times bring on his charm when he talked with Miss Emerson on the days he happened by and offered Melody a lift home from the schoolhouse.

The thought of school drew her eyebrows together in a frown. Should she help the teacher again? She had heard of a school in Faribault, a school for the blind. She wondered if she could be more useful there. She hadn't said anything to her parents, but it had been on her mind ever since Mrs. Larson, one of their well-meaning neighbors, had cornered her in the mercantile and suggested it to her.

"Melody! We're heading back now. You coming?"

"Coming, Harmony." Melody joined the others.

"Was that Jasper you were talking to?" Torkel asked. "Did he say if he's coming tomorrow to give us a hand?"

"Yes, he was on his way to speak to Dad. He'll be here."

Garrett spoke up. "I believe I met him in town."

Something in Garrett's voice made Melody wonder what the man thought of Ole Jasperson.

five

By 5:00 a.m. the next morning, Melody, her mother, and Harmony had the fire going in the stove, the coffee on, and breakfast underway. Her dad and brothers were taking care of the morning chores. First they fed and groomed the horses, milked the cows, and then took care of the pigs and chickens.

Breakfast came next. The Wheatlys were joined by the Rodwell men and Garrett as well as Jasper. Melody kept to the kitchen and refilled the bowls that kept coming back empty. They had potatoes, ham, eggs, biscuits and gravy, and Rommegrot, the cream mush that her father loved. When the men were well fueled for the day, they headed to the fields about 7:00 a.m. Josiah brought the new tractor over to help with some of the work, but most of the harvesting was done the old-fashioned way with the horse-drawn binder. The men shocked the grain, standing it upright in bundles as they moved about the field.

By 10:00 a.m. the horses needed a rest. Melody and the others, joined by Mina and her daughters had been working all morning to prepare the forenoon lunch. Beef and ham sandwiches on freshly baked bread, washed down with cold milk satisfied the men until they stopped again at noon to rest and feed and water the horses again.

Noon was the big meal. The women had been busy. They served ham and kumla, a potato dumpling boiled in the ham juices, sauerkraut, corn-on-the-cob, green beans, more fresh bread and jam, followed by pies and Fattigmand, a fried cookie. Melody enjoyed listening as the men praised the cooks. She heard Jasper explain the Norwegian kumla to Garrett, who seemed hesitant at first to try it.

Work continued in the fields until 4:00 p.m. when another big lunch was brought out to the men. More sandwiches, pies, and cookies kept the men going until they quit for the night and came in for supper.

A beef stew made with potatoes, carrots, rutabaga, root celery, root parsley, onions and leeks accompanied with more freshly made rolls and applecake for dessert completed the day. Garrett exclaimed over the stew, and Harmony told him it was another Norwegian favorite called lapskaus.

"I've never had such wonderful food. Your Norwegian dishes are excellent." He complimented the cooks.

"Just beware when Christmas comes and they serve you lutefisk," Jake warned. Melody could only imagine the horrified expression on his face by the laughter that followed.

"Well, if it's anything like today's fare, I welcome it." More laughter at Garrett made Melody smile. She also detected weariness in his voice. She heard Tobias stifle a yawn and someone else groaned as they stretched.

"It's been a long day and tomorrow will be another. I think we all better get some rest. Boys, evening chores are waiting." Keane slid his chair back.

"We need to do the same. Thank you, ladies, for the delicious food. The sight of you carrying baskets out to us was welcome relief." Melody could hear Jake pat his ribs. "But if I ate like this every day, I'd be as fat as a cow. How are you holding up, Garrett? Think you'd rather be at the mercantile instead?"

Garrett's reply was instant. "No, sir! I enjoyed every minute of the day."

Jake laughed. "We'll see how you feel about that in the morning. Muscles have a way of letting you know they haven't been used in a while."

Melody made her way to the kitchen after saying good-bye to the others. She checked the water temperature in the pot on the stove and found it hot enough to start dishes. She was about to lift the pot when she felt an arm brush hers.

"I'll get that for you, Mel. Look out there; it's hot."

She stood back. "Thanks, Jasper. You must be tired out too. It's been a long day."

"For you as well. I don't know how you women keep the food coming all day like you do, but I have to say, I wish it was harvest all the time because an old bachelor like me gets fed so well."

Melody smiled. "Will you be helping at your folks after your crops are in?"

"They're going at it right now and have plenty of help. I might drop in for a meal later though."

"You know you're always welcome to join us, Ole." Tuva stepped to the sink and set some dishes in the water. "Although you can be a bit selfish when it comes to food. I recall once when you wouldn't share a picnic basket with me."

Jasper laughed. "As *I* recall, it was a good thing I didn't. Seems to me you and Keane ended up sharing a lunch together. You should be thanking me."

Melody heard her mother give Jasper a hug. "I do. You were a blessing in a disguise. Now go home and get some rest. We'll see you back here tomorrow, bright and early."

"Yes, ma'am. Good night, Melody. Night, Harmony."

After Jasper left, the women put the kitchen to rights and started dough rising for the next day. Tuva had the meals planned out and Mina would bring in the side dishes. When the men worked the Rodwell farm, Tuva would bring the extras and Mina would do the main cooking. The system worked well. At Jasper's farm both women contributed.

"We'll have farikal tomorrow." Tuva checked her list. "I think the seasoned potatoes and carrots would go well with that."

"Yum!" Harmony finished putting the last dish away. "I wonder what Garrett will think of our farikal. Do you suppose he likes lamb?"

Melody shrugged. The dish was lamb and cabbage and black pepper. Surely it wouldn't satisfy everyone's tastes, but it was a favorite in their house. "Were you planning sørlandskompe for the next day, Mom? Dad would like that."

"Yes. We'll need to cook the salt pork the night before so it will be ready to be put in the potato ball. Okay then, doughnuts tomorrow too. Are you girls up to it? My feet are telling me it's time to get off them and into bed." Tuva kissed each of her daughters. "Good night, girls. Thank you so much for all your help today."

"Good night, Mom. Sleep well."

"Ready to go, Mel?" Harmony yawned.

"Soon. I want to get outside for some fresh air first. I'll be up shortly." Melody pulled her mother's shawl off the hook by the door and stepped outside. Her father and brothers were just coming in from the evening chores.

"The water on the stove is hot and ready for your wash-up." She told them.

"Thanks, Melody." Keane kissed his daughter on the forehead. "Don't stay out too long. You need rest too."

"Okay, Dad. Good night."

Alone at last, Melody strolled down to the row of pines. It was her favorite place on the farm. The open prairie didn't have much for trees when the settlers first came, but many had been planted around the farms for windbreaks. The huge cottonwood near their house was a rare sight. Of the trees in the area, most grew near the creeks or rivers. This tree was special. It held the sack swing that she and her siblings grew up enjoying. She still took a turn on it now and again when she thought no one was around.

The evening was cool and she felt the grass damp on her feet. It had been a fast moving day with all the cooking and cleanup to do, but she had enjoyed it. She liked feeling useful. There were so many things she could not do, so to contribute her efforts made her feel good.

She walked slowly down the path Jasper had made. Night walks didn't frighten her. To her it was always black, but she knew the difference and she understood the dangers that night could bring. Once she stumbled upon a skunk and got sprayed as a reward. She was about eleven then and Jasper was the one who found her, crying and sputtering as she tried to wipe the scent away. He got her home to her mother and laughed when she blamed the skunk, saying it should have been looking where it was going.

Melody's thoughts were interrupted when she heard a sound. She stopped where she was. She had no idea if there was moonlight or not, but she crouched down among the tall stalks of corn around her. She didn't know why, but she didn't want to be seen until she knew what the sound was. She listened again.

A creak of leather. Silence. Then a snort from a horse.

Melody's heart beat faster. There was someone on the road. Someone was just sitting on a horse, not moving. But why? Who?

Five or ten minutes passed, she wasn't sure, but finally the horse began walking. She clearly heard the hoofs hit the dirt and rock on the road. Whoever it was went by the house and kept going. When it was farther away, she heard the horse pick up speed.

Slowly Melody straightened. Her muscles hurt from being crouched down so long. She would tell her father about the strange incident, but not now. He would be asleep by now. She'd tell him in the morning.

She was troubled as she quietly prepared for bed. Harmony's even breathing meant she was already asleep, so she couldn't discuss what happened with her. It was very odd. The only other odd thing that had happened recently was the arrival of Garrett Foxe. Could the two incidents have something in common?

Melody slipped under the covers. On the table beside the bed was her Bible, a very special Bible written in Braille. She reached for it and using the special technique she had learned, she ran her fingers over the page as she continued her reading. "Be careful for nothing; but in everything by prayer and supplication with thanksgiving let your requests be made known unto God. And the peace of God, which passeth all understanding, shall keep your hearts and minds through Christ Jesus." The passage in Philippians was just what she needed. She turned her thoughts to prayer, giving her anxiety to the Lord. *"Give me wisdom too, Lord. Should I even think of moving from here to that school for the blind? Or should I stay and do what I can here? I don't want to be a burden on my parents all their lives. I need answers; help me to be patient."*

six

Jasper loved harvest time. The hard work exhilarated him, but it was seeing the fruits of his labor that was the real satisfaction.

He wasn't a rich man, but he had accomplished quite a bit in his thirty-one years. He paused with the rake in his hands as he studied his land. The Rodwell and Wheatly men had finished on their farms and were now lending their efforts to his crops. And they were good crops this year. He smiled with pleasure. He had bought the small farm that adjoined the Wheatlys about ten years previously. In that time he had restored the crumbling building that was once a barn and had torn down the rotting structure that had once been a house. A new house stood in its place.

His parents finally quit pushing him to marry and start a family. He had told them time and time again that when he was ready, he would. His younger brothers were married and producing grandchildren, so his parents had to be content with that.

He glanced over at Garrett Foxe. He was still uneasy about the man showing up after all these years, although it seemed that his reasons for being there were legitimate. Garrett made it clear that all he wanted was to know about his father and claimed he had no idea he had relatives here.

Keane told Jasper about the man on horseback Melody heard the other night, and Jasper couldn't help but wonder if it had something to do with Garrett. Jasper had waited night after night for any sign of the man and only ended up bleary eyed the next days from lack of sleep. He neither saw nor heard anyone around the Wheatly farm. Maybe it was nothing.

He heard the wagon coming and knew the women were bringing their lunch. The main meals were held at the Wheatlys' house even though Jasper had told Tuva she was welcome to use his, but she had stated that it was just easier to work in her own kitchen. He was fine with that. The break would be welcome and he watched the men gather round the wagon and he took his place among them.

"Lead us in prayer, will you, Jasper?" Jake asked.

Jasper's heart was full as he thanked the Lord Jesus for the blessings of food and friends and for the work getting done. "The crops are good, Lord, but you get the credit for that, not us. It's easy to be thankful when things go well. Help us to remember to thank you and praise you even when things don't go so well. In all things, may you get the glory. Amen"

Garrett's look was quizzical when Jasper glanced his way. It reminded Jasper that this was all new to the man. *"He needs you, Lord. Help me or one of the others to have the opportunity to share the Gospel with him."* That short prayer changed Jasper's perspective. He knew he had been viewing Garrett as an interloper with ulterior motives. Instead he needed to view him as a lost sinner in need of a Savior, just as he once had been.

"Thanks, Harmony." Jasper took the sandwich the young woman passed down to him from the wagon bed. He took the canteen of water and quenched his thirst before taking a bite. With his mouth full he managed to say, "It's good."

"'Course it is, Jasper. Nothing but the best for you." Harmony winked at him, and Jasper almost choked before he managed to swallow. The girl was getting far too cheeky for her own good. He grinned at Harmony and slid to the ground to lean against one of the wagon wheels. It offered a bit of shade as the fall day had heated up. He watched Harmony jump from the wagon to bring Josiah his lunch. She gave him a coquettish smile as well, and Jasper knew she would probably do the same with Garrett. But when she kept her eyes down and barely looked at the young man, Jasper was surprised.

Ah, so she feels a bit differently about Garrett Foxe! Interesting!

Maybe Harmony was finally growing up. She had been a flirt for so long that it was comical to see her tongue-tied around the new man.

She's so different from Melody.

Jasper knew Melody was still on the wagon handing out food to the others. He knew something was on her mind, but he didn't know what it was. He felt he knew her pretty well, but there were times she put up a hedge around herself and allowed no one to enter. She used to talk to him more when she was younger, but things changed somewhat when she became a young woman. Jasper just considered himself lucky to be her friend and confidant when she needed someone to talk to. If she had something to discuss with him, she would in her own time.

When Melody was born, it had shocked the small town to learn that she was blind. Jasper was only eleven at the time and had never been around someone who was blind. From the start he saw in her a determination to be like the people around her. She didn't want to be coddled, and it took some doing to finally get her to accept help of any sort. He remembered well watching her as a toddler walk into things and throwing a temper tantrum until she could get through a room without bumping something. Through patience Tuva and Keane taught her to put her arms out to feel ahead of herself, but she stubbornly refused to do so. After she had been knocked down enough times, she learned the room and could make her way through it without mishap. Jasper knew at that moment that she felt she had control of her situation.

It made him think of how easy things were for him. He had gone home and tied a kerchief around his eyes and left it there for days as he tried to maneuver his way around his home. His parents had finally put a stop to it when he nearly fell out of the hayloft. But it had given him an insight on her life. He understood her better.

Melody's brothers and Harmony were fierce protectors during her school years. Despite being blind, she attended school with the others and learned by listening. The teacher at the time got her some books in Braille and helped Melody to learn. Melody excelled. Her memory was amazing and she soon was the top student. It was also discovered that she had only to hear a song and she was able to play it on a piano. But the other students, not all, but some found ways to make her life miserable. Pranks and bullying were squelched by Melody's siblings, but it was Jasper, older and more intimidating, that put a stop to it. No one disrespected Melody or Jasper would hear about it.

He watched her now as she got off the wagon and carried a plate of doughnuts for the men to help themselves. They flocked around her nearly emptying the plate before she stepped over to him and knelt down with the plate extended.

"Want one, Jasper?"

He didn't know how she knew where he was, but she did. "No, I want two." He helped himself and grinned when he saw the satisfied smile on her face.

"I thought you would. She reached behind her back and held out another doughnut for him. "I saved this one for you. It's sugared, the way you like it."

"Why, thank you, ma'am!"

He got to his feet and gently took her elbow, leading her away from the others. In a more serious tone, he asked, "Any more midnight visitors?"

"Dad told you?"

"Yes. I don't know what to make of it. Maybe it's nothing. Maybe the man fell asleep for a while and then rode on."

Melody smirked.

"Hey, don't laugh. I've done it. But, seriously, Mel, maybe you shouldn't go out at night by yourself for a while."

She cocked her head to one side. "You worried about me?"

"No. I just don't want to have to clean you up again if another skunk sprays you."

Melody smacked him on the arm, and Jasper wondered how she knew exactly where to place her blow.

"Well, for your information, Garrett offered to come by later and take me for a walk." Her face revealed nothing to Jasper as she made this statement.

"I see." Although puzzled by this revelation, he kept his tone light. "You finally going to have a beau?"

Melody put a hand on her hip. "No, of course not. I think he asked Harmony too." She turned to leave then swung around, colliding with Jasper, who had also stepped forward. He caught hold of her arms and held them for a brief moment then dropped his hold. "Oh! Sorry! I just forgot to ask if you were going to be able to clean up enough to come to Torkel and Eve's wedding next week."

Jasper grinned and gave an exaggerated sniff. "What do you mean by that? Are you telling me I smell?"

"Yes."

"I see now why you don't have a beau yet, woman. You need a lesson in manners."

Melody laughed as she walked back to the wagon and joined Harmony and the others. Jasper followed with a grin on his face.

As the wagon bumped its way across the field, Garrett stepped to Jasper's side and watched it with him. "Uh, can I ask you a question, Jasper?"

"Sure." Jasper faced the man, knowing what he was about to be asked.

"I don't mean to pry, but are you courting one of the Wheatly girls?"

Jasper reached for his rake before answering. "No, they're just my friends, my *good* friends."

He waited for Garrett's nod before he moved on to his work.

Garrett heard the warning in Jasper's voice. He better not do anything to hurt the man's good friends. There was more to that warning than just friendship or Garrett knew nothing about human nature.

He picked up a rake and went back to work. His muscles had let him know they had been awakened after that first day of harvest. His arms had browned from being in the sun and the back of his neck had a sunburn that stung when his collar rubbed on it, but he was having a great time. Being a part of the Rodwell family was an experience like none other he'd ever had. He found their interest in him and care and attention something that he hadn't realized he'd been lacking. His mother tried, but she was always away at a job, trying to keep them in enough money for rent and food. There was never time for laughter and discussion such as he found in this household.

It was Josiah who encouraged him to ask Melody for a walk. At first Garrett wondered if Josiah wanted to keep him from asking Harmony, but his cousin claimed there was nothing but neighborhood friendship between him and the Wheatly girls.

"We've known each other all our lives, and if you ask me, Harmony can get a little too pesky, so don't be afraid to let her know if you're not interested."

Garrett was bothered by that statement, wondering what the young man had done to "let her know" *he* wasn't interested. He had seen Harmony try to walk with Josiah the first night they had gone to the Wheatly house. He recalled Josiah walking away, leaving Harmony, to Garrett's delight, to join the others.

But Melody also intrigued him. She was so capable and sure of herself. On the other hand, Harmony was completely enchanting with her outgoing personality. He found them both captivating. His experience with courting was minimal as there was never time or money for him to associate with a young lady. He still didn't have much for money, but he could afford the time to at least take a moonlight stroll with a beautiful young lady.

He washed up carefully after the evening meal and excused himself to head over to the Wheatlys. Jake and Mina knew his intentions and wished him a good evening. He felt a little nervous as he approached the door and saw Keane sitting at the table, his Bible open before him, a cup of coffee beside him.

Keane waved him in before he had a chance to knock.

"Come in, Garrett, come in." He waved Garrett to a chair. "I can't believe you have energy left for a walk, but that's youth for you. I remember the days. Melody will be down in a second. So, how do you like farming so far?"

The two men talked until Melody's footsteps sounded on the staircase. She walked into the room and Garrett got to his feet. Not wanting to make the situation awkward, he asked, "Are you ready, Melody?"

"Yes, be back soon, Dad."

"Sure, Mel. Have a good walk, you two."

Melody led the way to the door and Garrett watched her reach for a shawl on a hook before she stepped outside. She swung the shawl around her shoulders and turned to him.

"Where would you like to go?"

"Uh, well, what would you suggest?"

Melody appeared to be staring off into the distance, but Garrett shook that thought off as he reminded himself that she couldn't see anything. "I hear some crows out that way, so let's not go there. They might have found a dead rabbit or something."

Melody said it so matter-of-factly that it stunned Garrett. He had a lot to learn about country life. "Shall we go this way then?" He held out his arm to indicate the way and then felt foolish when she didn't turn with him.

"I know a spot. It's this way." She held out her arm, and Garrett realized that she knew what he had done and was copying him. Was she making fun of him?

They walked along in silence. Garrett was trying to think of something to say, but it was Melody who began.

"What do you think of the Rodwells?"

With relief, Garrett found his voice and they talked until Melody indicated that they were going to leave the road. "This is the tree where my mother would go every morning and sing as the sun came up," she told Garrett. Then she went on to explain how Keane heard her and came out in the mornings to listen to her.

"He didn't know who the singer was at first. He called her *bird girl* because it seemed that the birds joined in her songs." Melody reached the tree and took hold of a branch placing her foot in a notch and swung herself up to sit in the fork of two branches. "This is where she would sit while the sun came up." She pointed back down the road where a smaller tree stood. "That's where my father hid and watched her."

Garrett found a branch he could reach and pulled himself to sit on it. He looked down at Melody. "Thank you for telling me that. It must make this a very special place for you."

"It is special. Farther down this road is my grandparents' house, my mother's parents. She was the oldest of nine children, and my aunts and uncles are scattered all over Minnesota and North Dakota. We try to get together for a holiday or two, but it's hard for everyone to travel now and they are all so busy. It's sad when families grow apart."

Garrett watched her face with interest. She seemed to guard her emotions well, but he could see some sadness there. "At least you've had a family, and I bet yours won't go too far. You all seem very close."

"We are, and I'm very thankful for my family. I'm sorry you didn't have that when you were growing up." She changed the subject. "Do you think you'll stay in Minnesota now?"

Garrett shrugged. "I don't know yet, but I sure like it here."

"You haven't been through a winter yet. That might change your mind about it."

"Oh, but I've been in many Chicago winters, so you can't scare me with that."

Melody slid from the tree and Garrett joined her. "It's getting late; we should head back. In all seriousness, I should warn you that winters here can be deadly. Winds blow the snow across these fields and, excuse the expression, *blind* a person so that you don't know where you are and you don't know which way to go."

They started on the walk back. "You seem…I'm not sure how to say this…" Garrett stopped walking and Melody stood still and waited. "I've never been around a blind person before, and you seem…I guess what I'm trying to say is…you seem comfortable with it. I think I would be screaming at God to give me my sight. How do you do it?"

Melody's voice was quiet but she didn't falter in her answer. "I did scream at God, Garrett. Being born with blindness, I know no other way, and I was okay when I was a little girl at home. Then I went to school and it suddenly dawned on me that I was the only one who was blind. Everyone else could see, everyone else was the same, I was different. But I didn't want to be different."

She began walking again and Garrett kept pace with her, watching her face as she talked. "I was mad at God for making me different, but it was Jasper who helped me through that dark time. You see, I was not only in the darkness of blindness, but I was also in the darkness of sin. I was lost. Sure, I had heard Jake preach his sermons and tell us of salvation in Christ Jesus. I knew the Bible verses that said I needed to believe on the Lord Jesus Christ to be saved. I could tell others how to be saved. I knew it all. Then one day the frustration of blindness overcame me. I shouted, I yelled, I cried, and Jasper came to me and told me it wasn't God's fault. It wasn't my fault. It was the fault of sin, the sin I was born into in this world. He showed me that I was lost and on my way to hell unless I truly believed that Jesus died for *my* sin, and that Jesus lives again."

Melody stopped and turned to Garrett. "I was lost, Garrett, but now I'm found. I was blind, but now I see. I believed Jesus died for me that day, for my sin. I have no more reason to be angry with God for my blindness than you have for being raised without a father. It's the sin in this world that is the cause of all the problems we face, and we are part of that problem because we are sinners. But my sins were forgiven by the blood of Jesus Christ on the cross when I trusted in him. Yours can be too, Garrett."

Melody paused.

Garrett didn't know what to say. Never had anyone spoken to him in this way. Never had anyone told him he was a sinner.

"I'll be blind until the day I die or am called up to be with the Lord," Melody added. "But my blindness can't stop me from seeing and knowing about God's love for me. There's a verse in Ephesians that says God gives us 'eyes of understanding'. That's what we all need."

Garrett cleared his throat. "Thank you for telling me that, Melody. I'm sure that's a very personal story that you don't share with everyone."

Melody smiled. "Actually, I share it with everyone who will listen. It's a message that needs to be shared. Please think about it, Garrett. If you have questions, ask Jake or Mina or any of us. We will be happy to talk about it."

"Well, okay—"

Melody reached for Garrett's arm to stop him from moving on. "I mean it, Garrett. It's the most important decision you'll ever make in your life. It really is a matter of life and death. Will you spend eternity in heaven or hell?"

Later that night when Garrett was in bed, he thought about Melody's story. Her fervency caught his attention, but he couldn't help but think that because of her blindness she had taken on some sort of mission work. Why else would she spend half the night preaching to him?

He remembered Jake saying that in his father's dying breath he had believed on Jesus for his salvation. Jake said that Thorpe was in heaven now. Could that really be true? Could a man who had done the evil things Thorpe did really be in heaven?

seven

Chicago

Bill Gladstone looked up from his desk to check the time. It was nearly closing, but Mr. Wilson was still in his office. He glanced around the room. There were two other junior members of the law firm with desks like his out in the main area behind the reception desk, but the large offices that circled the room held the senior staff. Theirs bespoke grandeur and elegance, well befitting the status of their company. Only the wealthy could afford to do business with Wilson & Krause.

He busied himself with some papers in front of him when he heard the door open to Mr. Wilson's office.

"Good night. See you all tomorrow." The staff bid their boss a good evening. Once he was gone, the secretary tidied her desk and prepared to leave.

"Good night, Mr. Gladstone," she said to Bill.

"Good night, Mavis." Bill smiled to himself when he saw her frown. She disliked his informality with her and had asked him to use her surname. Bill did it just to annoy her.

The others left one by one until Bill was the last. "I'll lock up," he told one of his colleagues. Once the building was empty, Bill turned out the lights and locked the door, but he didn't leave. Instead he made his way through the dark building to Mr. Wilson's office. He knew where the paperwork was, and he needed to get some information from it.

Ulen

Melody was in the garden gleaning the last of what it could produce while she thought over the discussion she had with Harmony after her walk with Garrett.

"What did you talk about?" Harmony asked.

"Oh, I showed him Mom and Dad's tree and told how they met."

"What? I suppose he thought that was romantic."

"Romantic? Don't be silly. Wait. Are you interested in him?"

"Of course not!"

"That sounded like 'protesting too much'. Harmony, I have no interest in Garrett."

"Then why did he ask you instead of me?"

"You are interested!" Melody grew silent in thought. Was her sister finally serious about a man? *"Harmony, be careful. I gave Garrett my testimony, but he still doesn't see his need for the Lord."*

"I know." Harmony's voice was quiet. *"I've been praying, Mel. I've been praying!"*

Melody put her head up when she heard a horse on the road. She listened then rose with a smile.

"Grandpa Thomsen!" She called out. "It's about time you came for a visit."

"Hi Melody! Tell your mother to put the coffee pot on. I've got to bring this telegram down to that new fellow at Rodwell's first. Be back soon."

Melody listened as her grandfather walked the horse down the long driveway to their neighbor's. She headed back to the house, wondering who would be sending Garrett a telegram. From what he told them, there was no one in either Seattle or Chicago who was related to him.

"Mom, Grandpa Thomsen will be here soon." She explained to her mother the reason for the visit and quickly washed her hands so she could help prepare some refreshments. The house smelled delicious from all the baking she and her mother had been doing for Torkel and Eve's wedding which was to take place the following week.

"Will you call your father and brothers, please?"

"Sure." Melody stepped out the back door and reached for the bell hanging beside it. She tugged the rope and sent the bell to clanging. A couple of clangs was enough to let the men know that they were wanted at the house. A lot of clanging meant they needed to get there fast. The only time Melody remembered ringing the bell for all she was worth was when her mother was in labor with Tobias. She had been five at the time.

It wasn't long until all were seated around the table and Grandpa Thomsen was explaining his visit. "I was at the mercantile when Orris came in and asked Ole if anyone would be going out this way as he had a telegram for that Garrett Foxe fellow. I volunteered, figured it was about time for a visit with you folks anyway."

Melody took a sip of her coffee. Questions swirled in her mind about what the telegram for Garrett could be, and she wondered what Harmony was thinking, but she set her thoughts aside to listen to her grandpa. His visits always meant that there was news to share. Grandpa Thomsen always seemed to know what was going on.

No one spoke for a few seconds, and Melody wondered what was happening when her father started chuckling.

"Grandpa, what are you looking for?" Aslak's question made Melody even more curious.

"Just checking you boys out to see if you're infected."

"Infected!" Tuva exclaimed. "Don't tell me there's more cases of diphtheria."

"No, I'm afraid it's much more serious than that. There's a bad case of whiskerites in town. Seems like a lot of the young men have caught it."

Melody laughed with the others. She knew her father was clean shaven, and she suddenly wondered if Jasper had a moustache or beard. No one had mentioned it, and there would be no other way she would know.

Keane reached for a doughnut. "Any other major news to tell us, Pa?"

"Well, first off you should know that the Board of Health made a new law. Pigs are no longer allowed in the city limits."

"Good to know." Keane grinned and took a swallow of his coffee. "Reminds me when they ruled that cows couldn't be tied in the middle of the street anymore. Progress."

"I got some not so good news too." Melody listened as her grandpa stirred his coffee. He liked to add a little sugar and cream to it. "The Winnipeg Flyer hit the rear of one of the freight trains. The freight train wasn't moving, but it caused several other cars to derail. I guess the engineer and some of the other men jumped to safety, so no one got hurt. Could have been bad though."

Tuva gasped. "That's why I tell you boys to stay back from that train when it comes in. It makes me nervous to see children playing near those rails."

Grandpa continued. "There was a shooting over in Hagen."

"Oh, goodness! What now?" Melody heard her mother's fear.

"Some fellow got mad because someone else was bringing in bundles too fast during threshing and they got into a big argument, so the fellow went and got his gun and shot the other guy."

"He shot someone over that?" Tobias was incredulous.

"What's this world coming to?" Tuva got up to get more coffee. "Please tell me you don't have any more bad news."

"Well…"

Tuva sat down. "You do."

"Reiersgord found a skull in the Wiger pit when he went for a load of sand."

"A skull! You mean a human skull?"

"Yep. No way to tell how long it'd been there; could have been years and years. And speaking of finding things. Remember a couple of years ago when Hans Hanson found that old sword in his field while plowing?"

"Oh, I remember that." Aslak said. "Wish we'd find something interesting in our fields."

"Not a skull!" Harmony put in.

"What about the sword?" Keane brought the conversation back.

"Well, there's some professor that thinks it could be over five hundred years old and that it's likely Norwegian."

"Over five hundred years old? I'd say that's back when the Vikings came over."

Melody tuned out the excited discussion that followed that statement. Her mind was still on Garrett's telegram. What could it mean?

"Hey, who's that?" She heard Aslak go to the door. "Looks like Garrett is riding one of Jake's horses to town."

"Must be something to do with that telegram I delivered to him."

"You deliver telegrams now?" Tuva teased her father. "Quit staring out the door, Aslak. We'll find out what it's about if Garrett wishes to tell us. Now, Pa, are you and Mom ready for the big wedding next week? Can you believe your oldest grandson is getting married?"

"That's another reason I came this way." Grandpa drawled out the words, and Melody knew he had some big news to convey. It was so like her grandpa to hold back the biggest and the best for last. She heard him turn to Torkel. "You and your new bride are planning to live in that dinky little house over there, are you?"

Melody knew he pointed across the yard to the small house that had been made ready for the newlyweds.

"Yes..." Torkel leaned forward, trying to pull words out of his grandpa that would explain the reason for his question.

"Well, you can live there if you want, but I hear tell there's a good piece of farmland and a much larger house not far from here that's going for a good price."

"Where? I haven't heard of anything. Are you sure? There have been so many new families moving into the area that all the available places have been scooped up already. I've been looking at places closer to Hitterdal."

Melody smiled to herself. She thought she knew what her grandpa was up to.

"There's this old couple who find themselves rattling around in a big house with a bunch of empty rooms to clean, and they've decided it's too much for them to take care of anymore. The old farmer still likes to work the land, but his rheumatism acts up now and then and he thinks he could use some help..." Grandpa stopped talking and Melody guessed he was waiting for Torkel to catch on.

"Seriously? You'd sell us your place, Grandpa? Why, that would be great!"

"There is a catch to this deal, son."

Melody felt like everyone was holding their breath.

"You see, this old couple still needs a place to live, and they would really hate to leave the land, so they were wondering if you would be willing to move that little, dinky house over there onto their land and let them stay close by."

Melody heard Torkel's breath release in a whoosh. "Dad, what do you think? Could we do that?"

"Are you sure this is what you want, Pa?" Keane's voice was serious. "It would be quite a change for you and Ma."

"We're ready, son. When your bones creak louder than your rocking chair, it's time to make some changes. How do you feel about moving the little house?"

Melody forced a smile to remain on her face while the men discussed the new possibilities. Her dream of living in the little house once occupied by Ma and Pa Wheatly would not be possible now. She was happy, very happy for Torkel and Eve. It would be a dream come true for her brother who wanted nothing more than to farm and be near his family, but for her it meant continuing to live dependent on her parents. Maybe that job at the school for the blind was where she belonged after all.

"I have to go see Eve and tell her. Grandpa this is just great! I can't thank you enough." Melody heard Torkel hug their grandpa and then he raced out of the house and took off on a run.

It was very busy the next few days. The men set to work right away, jacking up the little house and putting beams under it. Josiah proudly hooked up their new steam tractor and almost effortlessly the little house began moving out of the driveway and down the road. The noise and excitement surrounding the doings helped Melody picture it in her head. Neighbors came to lend a hand and to see for themselves what a newfangled tractor was capable of. Jasper touched her arm and she turned to him.

"Kind of sad to see it go," he commented.

Melody walked with him away from the others.

"Something's bothering you, Mel."

"Oh, Jasper, I'm just being foolish. I'm really happy for Torkel and Eve starting out on their own place, and I'm glad Grandpa and Grandma will have the little house. It's just that...I had thought that one day I'd live in the house."

"You?"

"I need to try living on my own, Jasper. I don't want to be a burden to my folks all their lives. I thought that if I lived close by, I could still get help when I needed it, but that I wouldn't always be underfoot."

"Melody, you do beat all."

She stopped walking. "Why? Am I asking too much? I'm a grown woman, living with my parents. You know I'll never marry."

"Why do you say that?"

"Be honest with me, Jasper. Who would want a blind wife?"

There was no answer.

"See—" She started to say.

"Melody!" They were interrupted. "Hi, Melody. Hey, Jasper, could I steal Melody away for a minute?" Garrett strode over to them.

"Of course. I'll talk to you later, Mel."

Melody heard Jasper walk away. She turned to Garrett. "Yes?"

"I was hoping to get a chance to talk to you or Harmony today. She's not around, is she?"

Melody tried to hide her smile.

"I'm sorry, Garrett. She's in Flom getting her schoolroom set up. Can I help you?"

She heard Garrett sigh. "It's been so busy over at Jake and Mina's because of the wedding and now this house moving and all that I haven't been able to get away."

Melody felt Garrett take her arm and lead her toward the barn. She wondered if he wanted to continue their last discussion about salvation.

"I got a telegram a few days ago."

"Yes, I heard."

"It was the strangest thing, Melody. I've never gotten one in my life and it scared me. Who would be sending me a telegram? All it said was to call a phone number. So I went into town to use the phone and I called the number and it was a lawyer's office. He said that my *grandfather* just died."

"Your grandfather?"

Melody felt Garrett move and guessed he was nodding his head. "Yes! I told him that I have a grandfather here in Ulen but that was the only one I knew of. He said my grandfather's name was Gordon Fairfax and that he had lived right there in Chicago! Melody, I was astounded. I didn't know what to say. The lawyer said that I needed to go to Chicago to sign some papers, and that he had a packet for me left by my mother. My mother! I stammered something about not having the funds to travel to Chicago, and he said that he would send a man out here and asked where he could find me."

"So, someone is coming here with papers for you from your mother? And you had a grandfather in Chicago but your mother never told you about him or took you to meet him?"

"I am so confused by it all, Melody. Jake and Mina and I have discussed what it could all mean, but until the man comes, I just don't know what to think. I had no idea my mother had so many secrets."

"Maybe the lawyer will be able to answer your questions."

"I hope so. I haven't been able to sleep, wondering what it's all about."

They were quiet a moment. "What would you like me to do?" Melody asked.

"I was kind of hoping you'd tell Harmony, and I'd really like to have you and Harmony and your family be there with the Rodwells when I hear from this lawyer. I feel like you're all a part of this with me."

"I don't know if I can. School is starting—"

"Oh, surely they can get along without you for a day."

Melody didn't say anything.

"Thank you for listening to me." Garrett took her hand and gently squeezed it. "Shall I take you back to the house?"

"No, I'll stay here for now."

"Okay. I'll see you soon."

Garrett left and Melody made her way to the pines. *"Shall I take you back to the house?"* He still didn't understand that she could get around without help. *"They can get along without you."* Is that what everyone thought? Was her job at the school just a pity job, something to keep her busy?

Deep down Melody knew that wasn't true. She knew the students improved with her tutelage, but it hurt to have Garrett assume that she wasn't needed. Would she ever get over feeling useless? She shook off her depressing thoughts. This was a happy time for Torkel and Eve. She didn't want anyone to guess that she was battling with her own concerns. The verses she had read in Philippians came to mind again. She needed to give her requests to the Lord. There was nothing she couldn't talk to him about, and she smiled as she recognized that he already knew her thoughts before she brought them to him. Then she remembered that the verse said *with thanksgiving*.

Was she being thankful? It was easy to fall into despair when she looked at her situation, but that was not what God wanted her to do. She had heard well-meaning people make comments about her blindness like, "God is trying to teach you something" or "God caused this or that to happen to challenge you". But she knew better. She knew God taught her through his Word not through her circumstances. She could learn from her circumstances just as when she stubbed her toe or ran into something she learned that she needed to go in a different direction, but she also knew that how she *reacted* to stubbing her toe or running into something revealed what was inside her. If she reacted with anger and frustration, she wasn't depending on what God taught her in his Word. When she reacted with a thankful heart, relying on God to help her through her situations, she was pleasing the Lord. And that could only be done because she was saved and the Holy Spirit indwelt her.

She wasn't going to allow her concerns about being a burden depress her. She was going to rely on the Lord to see her through and direct her paths.

She felt better after reflecting on that truth.

Then there was her concern about Harmony's feelings for Garrett. Garrett needed the Lord.

eight

The September day was clear and warm. Sunshine flooded the room where Eve stood bedecked in her wedding finery before the mirror. Mina tried but failed to hold back tears while Naomi and Harmony described Eve's dress to Melody.

"She looks like a princess, Mel! There are pearl buttons sewn all down the back and lace around the neckline. Mom gave her an ivory brooch to wear, that's the something borrowed, and she's got a light blue hanky tucked up her sleeve for the something blue and for in case she starts crying. The dress is her something new, and for something old we have Grandma Helma's hair pins to hold her veil." Naomi rattled off all the requirements for her sister's bridal outfit.

"It sounds lovely. And it's satin, isn't it?" Melody smoothed her hand lightly over the skirt. "Torkel is going to be awestruck when he sees you, Eve."

"We better get going girls. Thank you so much for playing the piano today, Melody, and for singing with your mom and Harmony. I think I'm going to be crying through the whole thing!"

"Oh, Mom, stop or you'll have us all crying. Naomi, are you ready?"

"Ready!"

The ceremony was held outdoors in the Rodwell's yard. Families had been pouring in and were being seated on chairs and benches and hay bales covered with blankets. Everyone brought food for a potluck dinner afterward, but the Wheatly and Rodwell women had prepared all the baked goods, desserts, and wedding cake.

The piano had been brought over by wagon from the Wheatly's house and rested on the grass off to the side of where the ceremony was to take place. Melody had played for many weddings and funerals and never really felt nervous about it. Not being able to see the people probably helped keep her calm, but today she was aware of the crowd and the fact that this was her brother and best friend's day. Keane brought her to the piano as she was unfamiliar with how things were arranged. Once seated she placed her fingers on the keys and let the music flow from her. She felt her calmness return. She was thankful for the gift she had of being able to hear a song and play it. Music had been a great solace to her.

Harmony whispered to her when it was time for Naomi to begin down the makeshift aisle of grass and flowers. Jake and Eve followed. When they were all assembled, Harmony let her know to end her song.

Melody stayed at the piano through the ceremony. When it was time for her mother and Harmony to join her, she played and sang with them.

> *All the way my Savior leads me;*
> *What have I to ask beside?*
> *Can I doubt His tender mercy,*
> *Who through life has been my Guide?*
> *Heav'nly peace, divinest comfort,*
> *Here by faith in Him to dwell!*
> *For I know, whate'er befall me,*
> *Jesus doeth all things well,*
> *For I know, whate'er befall me,*
> *Jesus doeth all things well.*

They sang through to the last verse and there was a stillness when they were done as if the chirping birds had stopped to listen to them as well. Jake pronounced the couple married, and Melody waited for the crowd to finish clapping before playing the recessional and a few other pieces as people began visiting and congratulating the couple. She got up and stood by the piano bench, wondering which way to go so that she didn't bump into anyone, when she felt a hand on her elbow. She smiled.

"Hi Jasper."

"How do you always know? Is it the soap I use or what?" She heard Jasper sniff as if checking his scent.

She laughed. "I'll never tell. What did you think of the wedding, you old bachelor?"

"Ouch! She strikes again!" Jasper pulled Melody's hand through his arm. "The wedding was very nice. I like the way Pastor Jake uses the opportunity of having a captive crowd to share the Gospel. There are many here from town who don't attend church and maybe have never heard."

Melody nodded. She liked that Jasper found that important.

"You look nice today, Melody."

Melody put her hand to her heart as if in shock. "Why, thank you, kind sir! And what attire do you have on?"

"Not my bib overalls."

They laughed. Then Melody turned to Jasper. "Can I ask you a silly question?"

"Of course."

"Do you have whiskers?"

"What?"

"Grandpa said that the young men in town were all growing whiskers for some strange reasons, and I wondered if you had any."

"Well, you tell me."

Melody hesitated. Jasper reached for her hand and slowly directed it to his face. Very lightly Melody ran her fingers across his chin and upper lip. His skin was smooth and his lips well defined. She pulled away quickly and her voice shook a little when she spoke. "No. Good! I'm glad. Dad is clean-shaven too."

"For all you know I have a wart on my nose."

"You do not! Harmony would have told me."

"Oh? How has Harmony described me to you?"

Melody smiled. "Never you mind. Take me to the food. I'm hungry."

Jasper assisted her through the food line. Her mother and Mina had a bevy of women who insisted on taking on the serving so that they could be with their guests. Melody was thankful to just sit and enjoy hearing the conversations around her. The sun felt warm and she turned her face toward it. There wouldn't be many warm days left.

"Hi Melody. This is Garrett."

Melody lowered her head to hide her expression at his announcement of his presence as Garrett joined her. Jasper had gone to get her some lemonade.

"Hello, Garrett. I guess we're almost related after today."

"What? How's that?"

"Well, Torkel is my brother and Eve is your cousin. That must relate us in some way." She only meant to tease Garrett, but he didn't seem to catch on.

"Does it work that way? I mean, you're not my cousin now, are you?"

She laughed. "No. Eve is my sister-in-law now. That's all. Did you enjoy the wedding?"

Relief came through Garrett's voice when he answered. "I did. I can honestly say that I've never been to one before. I didn't know there would be preaching involved. Your song was really beautiful, by the way. Your voices—they are really something."

"Thank you, Garrett. I especially like the words of that song because they were written by a blind woman named Fanny Crosby."

"Oh, I see."

Melody sensed that Garrett was uncomfortable with the subject, so she asked. "Have you heard when the man from Chicago is coming?"

"No, nothing more. I'm quite nervous to find out my mother's reasons for keeping her secrets. Why wouldn't she want me to know that I had a grandfather? Was he cruel to her? After learning the terrible things about Thorpe Prescott, I'm almost afraid that there's more bad news in store for me. Sometimes I wish I had never sought answers."

"No, I don't believe that. You would always wonder if you hadn't, so it's best to find out. I've been praying for you, Garrett."

"You have? Why? I mean, what have you been praying for?"

Melody was careful in her answer. "I've been praying that you'll come to see your need of accepting the Lord Jesus as your Savior and that you'll find peace in the answers you've been seeking."

"Oh, well, thanks."

Jasper returned to Melody's side, and she reached out her hand to take the glass of lemonade he said he'd get her. He handed it over with a chuckle. "You just pretend to be blind, don't you, Melody!"

Garrett gasped beside her. She felt him stand. "Excuse me, please." His voice had an icy tone.

Jasper took the seat beside her. "I don't think that fellow thought I was funny. He glared at me like he'd like to punch me."

Melody smiled. "He just doesn't understand our relationship."

Jasper leaned closer. "We have a relationship? I'm shocked! I never knew!"

"Oh, go play horseshoes or something. You're bothering me, old man."

"That's right!" Jasper stood. "I have my championship title to defend. I'll see you later."

"Okay, but I won't see you."

Jasper laughed. He left her smiling at his antics. Not everyone understood Jasper like she did, and even she thought him a mystery at times. According to Harmony, Jasper was a sought after bachelor in the area, good looks and all, but he never talked about seeing anyone. She still wondered if he was sweet on Miss Emerson.

Thinking of the schoolteacher, Melody wondered if she were in the crowd. She had stopped by the house one day and they had gone over some lesson planning to prepare for the school year. Melody had hesitated about asking, but she finally got up the nerve and asked Miss Emerson if she were truly a help to her or if she was just given the job to give her something to do.

"Are you seriously doubting your effectiveness, Melody? I rely on you so much that sometimes I think you do more of the teaching than I do. I seem to be kept busy keeping the children from misbehaving while you get them to the actually studying. Don't ever think I don't need you."

It made Melody feel better and helped her decide to continue this year at the one-room school. Perhaps next year she'd look into going to Faribault, if the school for the blind would accept her as a helper there.

People were talking all around her. Melody grew weary of staying in one spot, but it was easier to have people come to her to visit than for her to try to bump her way through the crowd. She could hear some beginning to call their families together to leave and some wagons started down the driveway. She heard the swish of satin and stood as Eve and Torkel came to her.

"We're leaving now, Melody. Thanks again for all that you've done. Please come to visit us soon."

"Not too soon," Torkel teased. "I want some time alone with my wife." He reached for his sister and hugged her. "I'll miss you, Mel."

For the first time that day Melody felt tears sting her eyes. It suddenly hit her that Torkel would no longer be in their home. Tomorrow Harmony would be leaving for the school in Flom. No doubt she'd marry before long, then how many more years until Aslak and Tobias left? Things were changing too quickly.

She managed to steady her voice and smile. "Best wishes to you both. I love you."

A quick hug from Eve and they were gone. Melody stood listening to the well-wishers sending them off. All she wanted to do was to go home and have a good cry, but there were things to do to clean up after the guests. She listened for her mother's voice and headed in her direction.

Jasper pulled the quilt closer around his shoulders. The nights were getting cooler; he'd be lighting a fire soon. He closed his eyes and tried to sleep, but all he could think of was the moment when Melody had touched his face. It had taken will power to resist taking her in his arms right then and there and tell her how he felt about her.

He didn't know for sure when he fell in love with Melody. She had always been special to him, her blindness partly the reason. But as she got older and the rapport between them grew, he knew she was special in a different way. She was the woman he hoped would one day agree to be his wife.

Her blindness was no deterrent to him. Melody was complete in every way and would always be so to him. She was kind, she was funny, she was witty, she was absolutely beautiful, and she loved the Lord. He felt incomplete without her, but he couldn't let her know how he felt. Not yet.

He rolled onto his back and flung an arm over his head. She didn't see him as a suitor. To her he was an old friend. The years between them made her treat him like a doting uncle. He didn't know how to change that without driving her away from him. He didn't want to risk losing the closeness they had. If she found she could not return his feelings, they would never have the same relationship again. He didn't know if he could handle that.

Garrett was a concern. He was interested in Melody or Harmony, Jasper didn't know which. When Jasper heard that he had taken Melody for a walk, he had been worried, more worried than he cared to admit even to himself. He was shocked when Keane came up behind him the day they moved the little house and said, "You've been waiting a long time for Melody, Jasper. When are you going to let her know how you feel?"

He spun around and stared at the man. "You knew?"

Keane grinned. "I think I've known longer than either of you. You and Melody belong together."

Jasper studied Keane. "But you can see that she doesn't think of me like that."

"Not yet. But she will. You have to let her know." He squeezed the younger man's shoulder.

"You'd be okay with that? You don't think I'm too old for her?"

Keane laughed. "No, I don't think you're too old. I do think you're a bit slow though." He walked away chuckling.

He made it sound so easy. Jasper knew Melody well, but he didn't know if he revealed his feelings to her if she would run to him or away from him.

"Lord God, you said I could bring all my requests to you. You know what my request is, but if Melody and I are not to be together, if that is not your will, help me to let her go."

nine

Ulen

Bill Gladstone got off the train and looked in disgust at the little town. His suit was dusty from travel and he was tired and cross. He had barely spoken to his traveling companion, Donald Casper, another apprentice at the firm, because he was angry that he couldn't make this trip alone. When he had presented his argument for going by himself to the senior partners, he emphasized the expense it would entail to send two men, but even though Mr. Wilson had been agreeable, Mr. Krause had reminded him of company policy.

    He approached the station man and asked for a ride to be called to bring them to the hotel. The man looked at him as if he were addled.

    "The Orient Hotel is just down the block." He looked the two men over. "Unless you got some reason you can't make it that far, I suggest you walk."

"Thanks." Bill sneered. He stepped off the platform and looked both ways.

"To your right," the station man called behind him.

Bill didn't even bother to see if Casper followed him. He headed in the direction of the hotel. Only two motor cars were on the streets, he noted. Horses and buggies or wagons seemed to be the popular mode of transportation. He felt like he had taken a step back in time.

The hotel was nothing like what he was used to. The man behind the counter greeted the visitors by holding out his hand. Bill hesitated then shook the portly man's hand, wiping his hand on his pant leg afterward. The man raised an eyebrow.

"Name's Knute. If you'd just sign here, I'll get you your keys. I see you won't need help with your bags, so if there's anything else, you just holler."

"Thanks, I will."

Bill gave the lobby a brief perusal before taking to the steps. Before Casper left him to go to his own room, Bill said, "We can meet for breakfast. I'm going to have a look around the town then get to bed early."

Donald Casper acknowledged with a short nod of his head. Apparently he'd had enough of his rude colleague. He shut the door behind him.

Bill shrugged and entered his room. It was adequate. Just. He checked his watch. It was still early enough that he should be able to meet with his contact and get things underway. If all went well, he should be out of town by this time tomorrow and on his way back to Chicago. He went to the wash bowl, shaking his head that there was no indoor plumbing, and loosened his collar. A quick swipe over his face and neck and a rinse of his hands and he felt better. He locked his room and made his way down the steps, past the man named Knute who was now fast asleep with his feet propped up on the desk, and headed outside. He looked up and down the street until he located the livery stable, something which was almost obsolete in his business district. He tried to act natural as he walked down the boardwalk, but it seemed that everyone took notice of him. Many greeted him, wished him a good day, or just nodded. It would be difficult to go unnoticed in this place.

He rented a horse and buggy from a man named Stende at the livery. He wasn't about to ride horseback in the clothes he was wearing. There was a road south out of town and he headed that way. He thought he'd just walk the horse until he was out of sight, but the flat land stretched for miles and he wondered how far he would have to go before he couldn't be seen. Then he realized that the land did dip and raise slightly, so that the buildings of town finally disappeared. There was a crossroad up ahead and Bill stopped and waited there. He looked in all directions, but could see nothing. Was the man going to fail him now? Then, as if out of nowhere, a rider came toward him. Bill searched behind the man but could not see where he could have been hiding.

"Gladstone?" The man asked. He looked like a farmer with a wide brimmed hat, flannel shirt and jeans. Could this possibly be the right man?

"Lee?"

The man nodded and waited for Bill to speak again.

"Well. What have you found out?" Bill's impatience was evident.

"He calls himself Garrett Foxe. He's staying with a family named Rodwell. It appears that Mrs. Rodwell is his aunt on his father's side. He has grandparents here and cousins too."

"That won't matter. It's his mother's side we're concerned about."

The man nodded again.

"About how old would you say he is?"

Lee took off his hat and scratched his head, as Bill watched with distaste. "I'd say mid-twenties."

"Did you get a good look at him? Does he resemble Gordon Fairfax at all?" Bill pulled a picture from inside his coat and showed it to Lee.

"Can't say that he does. I got a good look at him 'cuz they had a wedding at their place and I sort of joined in."

"A wedding? He didn't get married, did he? That would change everything."

"No, it was his cousin."

Bill looked at him curiously. "You went to the wedding?"

Lee shrugged. "They invited the whole town. There's lots of new people here, so I figured they wouldn't know the difference."

"I don't like you taking chances on being recognized later. Okay, meet me somewhere by their place after I go see him. Once the papers are signed, you can do what I pay you for."

"Yes, sir. There's a little white schoolhouse not far from their place if you take the road south. I'll meet you there."

"See that you do. Good night."

Lee made no answer, just turned and walked his horse away. Bill watched him then turned his horse and buggy around. When he looked back, Lee was gone.

Harmony was more nervous than she had ever been when she looked at the fifteen faces staring up at her. Then her teacher instinct kicked in and it was as if she had been doing it all her life. The school day fled by and though weary at the end of it, she felt she had been successful. It was going to be a good year.

She closed the schoolroom door and headed down the steps only to falter when she saw Garrett leaning against the side of the building. He straightened when she looked at him, and she knew in that instant how much she had missed him, although it had only been a day since seeing him.

Her heart beat faster as she waited for him to walk to her.

"Hello, Harmony. Josiah had to come to Flom to speak to someone, so I asked to tag along so I could see you."

Harmony's voice was quiet. "You wanted to see me?"

"I didn't get a chance to talk with you at the wedding, and you weren't around the day the house was moved. I did talk with Melody, but it was you I wanted to talk to."

Harmony waited. "I thought…I thought you and Melody…" She hugged her schoolbooks to her chest as if keeping a wall between her and Garrett.

Garrett seemed puzzled until understanding hit him. "Oh! No, no, it's nothing like that. I like talking to Melody because she's easy to talk to, you know, like a sister. I…I seem to get all tongue-tied around you." He looked sideways at her.

Harmony couldn't contain the smile his words brought to her.

"May I walk with you to wherever you're going?"

She nodded and when he reached for her books, she hesitated before handing them over. Garrett held out his arm, and she looked into his eyes before slipping her hand into it.

Garrett cleared his throat and began to explain about the telegram and the phone call. "I don't know what this lawyer has to tell me, Harmony, but I sure would like it if you were there to hear it with me. I've learned a lot and I'm really happy to have found my family. I'm afraid bad news is on the way, and I need all the support I can get."

"I'll be there, but…Garrett, no matter what the news is, you will always have your family here. The Rodwells will stand by you."

"Will you, Harmony?"

"Yes. Yes, I will."

It was the next day that Bill Gladstone showed up at the Rodwell farm. He drove the rented buggy from the night before, leaving Donald Casper to follow on horseback.

"You don't mind, do you, Don? I met a girl last night and I figured as soon as we're done with Prescott, I'd make a call on her."

Donald made no reply, but it was evident that he was fed up with his coworker's behavior.

One look at Bill Gladstone and Garrett recognized his type at once. Walking the streets of Chicago, Garrett had wandered into the business and wealthy districts a time or two and had seen the young businessmen in their suits and ties. Though he was their same age, the businessmen had looked down their noses at the man in worn, dusty clothes, who was out of place in their world. The man who knocked on the door of the Rodwell home was probably in his early thirties. He entered and looked at the people there in much the same way as those businessmen had looked at Garrett. Garrett was suddenly glad that there had been no warning of his coming that day. It was just as well that Melody and Harmony were not there. Behind Mr. Gladstone came another man, and Garrett saw a sharp contrast in the two men. When introduced, Donald Casper spoke politely and shook hands all around. Mina invited their guests in while Jake sent Josiah to get Tuva and Keane to join them. All the younger children were also at school.

  Jake and Mina welcomed their visitors and asked them into the living room. Mina offered refreshments and was refused, so they all sat down, explaining that they would like to wait for the neighbors to join them. Garrett wondered what the city men thought of the reason, but he didn't care. Right now he felt he needed all the support he could get.

They made small talk until the Wheatlys arrived. Once everyone was gathered and introduced, Mr. Gladstone began.

"Do you have proof that you are the man named Garrett Foxe Prescott?"

There was silence as all eyes turned to Garrett. "I've only known my name to be Foxe. Do you need to see the birth certificate I have?" Garrett narrowed his eyes at the young lawyer.

"Yes, of course. I need to see any paperwork you have that proves you are who you say you are."

"Well then. Please excuse me a moment." Garrett rose to go upstairs.

The others waited quietly until Jake spoke. "We have no doubt in our mind that Garrett is my wife's nephew. His resemblance to her brother and father is uncanny."

"It is not the relationship with his father that I care to corroborate, it is his mother's heritage that requires proof."

The others looked at Mr. Casper after Mr. Gladstone's curt reply, but the man made no comment.

Nothing more was said until Garrett returned and handed some papers over to Mr. Gladstone. "As you can see, Mr. Gladstone, there is my birth certificate as well as my mother and father's marriage certificate."

The man looked over the papers. "This proves your legal name is Prescott. Did you never question your mother's maiden name?"

"I guess I never took notice. I only saw the papers a couple months after my mother's death and the first thing I saw was my father's real name. I came here to find out who he was and I found I had relatives here."

"Well, you had them in Chicago too. Your mother never told you this?"

"No."

"You had no idea Gordon Fairfax was your mother's father? Her maiden name is listed right here on the marriage certificate—Adele Fairfax."

"I never thought—"

"Are you sure you have no other siblings?"

"You mean brothers or sisters? No, it was just my mom and I."

"But are you sure? Your mother lied to you about so many things, how could you be sure about that?"

"Now, hold on! You have no reason to talk about my mother—"

Jake held out his hand. "Let's slow down and talk about this reasonably." He motioned for Garrett to sit down as he had started to rise from his chair. "Garrett has told you all he knows. What information do you have for him?"

Bill Gladstone set down the papers that Garrett had shown him. He reached into the briefcase by his side and pulled out some other papers.

"Adele Fairfax was the only child of Gordon and Edith Fairfax. The family lived in Chicago. At eighteen Adele married Thorpe Prescott against her father's wishes. She was immediately disinherited and her father cut all ties with her. She and her husband left Chicago and she was never heard of again until she came to the office of Wilson & Krause a little over three months ago. Edith Fairfax died a couple years after Adele disappeared.

"Her visit to our office caused quite a stir because the firm had been hired to locate her and had been attempting to do so for the past twenty-five years."

"Twenty-five years! But that's how old I am!" Garrett was puzzled.

Mr. Gladstone continued as if he hadn't been interrupted. "As soon as Gordon Fairfax realized his daughter had disappeared, he regretted his decision to disinherit her and he began searching for her. The man Thorpe Prescott was discovered, but there was no explanation of where Adele was. It was believed she had died."

"There had to be a reason she changed her name." Mina said softly.

Mr. Gladstone nodded his head in acknowledgment. "It is believed that she feared for her life. We do not know if she discovered her father's change of heart or not, but it is believed that she feared her husband would somehow get his hands on her inheritance if he knew where she was."

The lawyer again reached into the briefcase as if searching for something. He spoke quietly to Mr. Casper who frowned at him. Mr. Casper got to his feet, but it was Bill Gladstone who spoke. "You'll have to pardon me, but I forgot some paperwork in the buggy. Mr. Casper will retrieve it for me."

The other lawyer left the room.

Mr. Gladstone quickly pulled some papers out of the briefcase. "I will need you to sign these statements verifying you are Garrett Foxe Prescott and that you have no knowledge of any siblings and that if indeed siblings were discovered, the inheritance would be equally shared with them, the total of which would go to them and to your own heirs upon your death."

The words were rattled off and papers shoved in front of Garrett one after another. The lawyer took out a pen and started pointing to the places Garrett should sign.

"Inheritance?"

Garrett was stunned by the news and shuffled the papers before him.

"Excuse me a minute. Garrett, you need to read those before you sign." Jake suggested.

Bill Gladstone pulled out his pocket watch. "I'm sorry to rush you. I do wish to catch the train. If you would just sign here…and use your complete name, please."

Garrett took the pen, dipped it in ink, and began signing the papers.

Jake and Keane looked at each other. Something was not right. They looked up as Mr. Casper returned, seemingly agitated.

"There weren't any papers in the buggy," he accused his business partner.

"Oh, that's right! They were all here. Well, our business here is done."

Mr. Casper picked up the briefcase and looked inside. "You forgot to give Mr. Prescott this." He pulled out a leather pouch and handed it to Garrett. "Your mother left a packet with Wilson & Krause with instructions for it to be given to her son Garrett Foxe Prescott upon her death. This is the packet your mother left for you. Please verify that the seal has not been opened."

Garrett took the pouch and checked the seal and the date. He nodded to the man who jotted something down on a notebook. "What do I do now? Do I open it?"

"You may open it now or at your leisure. You may wish for privacy to do so." Mr. Casper held out his hand to shake Garrett's. "May I express condolences on the deaths of your mother and your grandfather, and I would like to congratulate you, Mr. Prescott, on your inheritance. Be assured that Wilson & Krause will do the utmost to help you invest and protect your fortune."

"My…fortune?"

Mr. Casper frowned at Bill Gladstone before nodding in the affirmative to Garrett. "Gordon Fairfax had sizable wealth."

ten

Melody stood with the children while Miss Emerson read the Scripture. She could hear the rustling of fabric as the girls smoothed their skirts and the shifting of feet as the boys took their positions. There was a lot of scraping of shoes on the wood floor as the children sat down. It was the first day of another year and Melody felt excitement at being a part of it. She did love working with the students and helping them learn. There were new children in the room this year and she'd do her best to understand their needs. She already had plans on how to help the ones she worked with the previous years.

The day flew by. She had a desk in the corner where one student came at a time and read to her. She knew the readers by heart and could help when a child stumbled over pronouncing a word. She emphasized the sounds of the letters and had them repeat them to her. It was new for some of them to have a blind lady help them with reading, but Melody knew that they would become accustomed to it.

She was tired when the day ended. She could tell that Miss Emerson was too by the way she bid the children farewell. Melody heard her slump into her chair with a big sigh.

"I think we'll have our work cut out for us this year, Melody. Some of the new students only speak Norwegian and they look so lost. It helps that you can communicate a little with them."

"Thankfully my grandparents taught me enough to get by, and we do have some of the readers in both Norwegian and English, so they'll catch on eventually. I hope they help their parents learn some English at home."

"Well, I'm exhausted. I'm sorry that we don't live in the same direction or I'd be happy to give you a ride."

"No problem. Jasper made a path for me from the schoolhouse, through his yard, and onto my house. It cuts down the distance by about half a mile, so I really don't have too far to go. Besides, I've been longing to get outside as much as the children have today. I told Aslak and Tobias to go on ahead as they have chores to do."

Miss Emerson laughed. "It is hard to get them to pay attention when the sun is shining. Good night, Melody."

"Good night."

There were still several things Melody wanted to take care of before the next school day, so she set to work to prepare. She wondered how Harmony had done the day before when school in Flom began. She already missed her nightly conversations with her sister and her detailed descriptions of the happenings of the day.

She was just about finished when she heard a horse and buggy stop in the schoolyard. She wondered if one of the parents had come to talk to the teacher.

As she headed to the door she heard another horse walk down the road and stop. There was a creak of leather as a person shifted position in the saddle and she could hear the horse side step and paw the ground. Melody thought nothing of it and reached for the door.

"Okay, Lee. I got Garrett Prescott to sign the papers, so my part is done."

The man's voice stopped Melody. It was no one she was familiar with, so she listened, unaware that she was holding her breath. *Garrett...Prescott?*

"When do you want him killed?"

The words hit her like a blow. *Killed? Garrett? They're going to kill Garrett?*

Thoughts of what she should do raced through her mind. She needed to warn Garrett. She needed to hear what else they had to say.

She needed to stay hidden. They must not know she is there.

She suddenly remembered the schoolroom windows and crouched down.

She could hear them speaking again.

"Make it look like an accident. I don't want any investigations or the deal may fall through. Prescott doesn't have any relatives left on his mother's side, but the papers he signed say that if there were any, the inheritance from old man Gordon Fairfax would go to them after Garrett Prescott's death."

"But you said there weren't any more relatives."

The man laughed. "I've got Lorna Landly, a very convincing actress, who will claim she was Garrett's sister, and I'm a good enough lawyer to have all the *legal* papers to back her claim. Lorna will get a share of the money, you'll get your share, and I'll get mine."

"Sounds easy enough."

"Easy? It's been a lot of work, my friend. It's taken the firm years to find the daughter of Gordon Fairfax. I thought I could put my plan into effect with her death, but I didn't know then about the son. There's been nothing easy about it. Even this trip has been a fiasco with the firm insisting on sending Casper with me. At least he didn't look over which papers were signed, but it will be worth all the trouble if you can do your job right."

"Consider it done."

Melody felt her mouth grow dry while she waited. She dared not move in case she made a noise that would attract the men's attention.

"You sure this schoolhouse isn't being used? There seems to be an awful lot of tracks around here."

"I've been sleeping in it off and on, so I know no one's been here."

Suddenly the first man's voice raised in anger. "You idiot! That's because school hadn't started yet. When does it start? You better go check it out and make sure there's no one there. I don't like all these tracks here."

Melody's heart raced. There was no place to hide in the one-room school. She had to move now before the man came around to the side of the building where the door was. She could hear the saddle leather creak as he got off the horse.

She had to move now. Melody opened the door just enough to slip through and left it as she tiptoed down the steps and ran to the side of the building. She could only hope that the other man was back far enough on the other side not to see her as she pressed herself against the school house.

She heard footsteps as the man climbed the stairs and pushed the door open. She heard him come back and stand as if he were looking around then his footsteps ran down the stairs.

Did he see me?

She heard him run back to the other man. She had to get to a better hiding place, but where? *The outhouse!* With no time to think things through, she ran as quietly as she could to the little building behind the school. She wasn't on the normal path where by the feel of the ground beneath her feet she could tell where she was, so she had to run with her arms outstretched in the general direction, hoping to find the little structure. She swung her arm wide and hit something solid. She felt for the rough wood and patted her way around it so she was hidden behind it. Her breath was coming in gasps and she tried to stifle it to hear what was happening. The men's voices were raised.

"Someone's been there…door open…papers and such…better look around."

Melody only had a moment before the man came back to this side of the building. She knew her hiding place would be discovered and she decided to run for it. When Jasper made the path for her, he left a couple rows of corn stalks standing on either side of it to help her find her way. Melody ran toward the path until she felt the cornstalks then she dove to the ground and lay as still as she could hoping the movement of the stalks would be attributed to the wind.

She tried to remember what she was wearing. It was the brown skirt and a brown jacket over her white shirtwaist. She breathed in relief. If it had been the blue skirt it would have shown up in the corn. By now the corn should be withered and brown, so maybe she blended in. She was suddenly thankful for Harmony pairing up her outfits and sewing a different size button on the inside to indicate the color for her when she dressed each morning.

She had no way to know if she was visible or not. All she could do was lie as still as possible and hope the man didn't see her.

"Where does that path lead?" The first man's voice was hard to hear and she guessed that he still was in his buggy. She knew she was right when she heard him snap the reins and move closer.

"I think it's just a path kids take to walk to the school."

Melody nearly started when the man spoke. He was very near.

"No one seems to be around." She heard him open the outhouse door and walk around it. Then footsteps moved away, back toward the school.

"You better be right. Mistakes like this could ruin everything. Now here's what you need to do."

Melody strained to hear more, but the men had moved away. She stayed still, not heeding the grasshoppers that jumped into her hair or the cramping of her muscles as she tensed in fear. She stayed that way until she heard the buggy leave and was sure it was far down the road.

Where is that other man?

Melody hadn't heard him leave unless he left at the same time as the first man. She may have missed hearing the horse over the noise of the buggy. Was he still in the schoolyard?

She had to take a chance. Garrett's life was in danger and she had to let someone know who could warn him. She got up very slowly to a crawling position and felt her way through the cornstalks to the open path. Getting her feet under her, she kept low to the ground and took off down the path, trying not to disturb the stalks too much, but she had to keep her hand out to feel where they were and she knew she was bumping them. Her mind was telling her that if the man was there and saw the stalks moving, he'd know she was there. She had no way of knowing how visible she actually was.

Once around a bend in the path, she believed she was out of sight of the school. Melody raced for all she was worth. If only she could get to Jasper's house, she'd be safe. She was gasping for air when she felt the stalks no longer on either side of her. She was in Jasper's yard. She went straight to the house and felt along the building until she found the door. She burst inside.

"Jasper! Jasper! Help!"

There was no answer. She nearly cried in frustration. She made herself listen even though she was breathing hard. Silence. Then, very faintly, she heard a horse on the road. Had she been seen after all? Should she try to get to her parents' house or should she hide? If the man had indeed seen her, she'd never outrun him now with him being on horseback. But where could she hide?

She had never been in Jasper's house. It wouldn't have been proper for a young lady to visit a bachelor in his home. But now was no time to think of that. She began feeling her way around the room. She stopped suddenly as an odd feeling came over her.

Instead of waving her arms as she had been doing, she moved purposefully across the room and reached out and touched the counter. She felt her way down to the water pump then across to the stove. She turned to the ice box.

Was her mind playing tricks on her? This was her mother's kitchen! But it wasn't. Some things were different. Her hand reached up and opened a cupboard and she lightly ran her hand over the dishes, cups and glassware. It was all there. She bent to the stove and felt for the frying pan her mother kept there. There was a frying pan, but it felt as if it had never been on a fire, shiny and new.

What was this? Was she in some sort of dream or nightmare? Her head came up with a start. A horse was coming into the yard.

No, this was real. For some reason she didn't understand, Jasper's kitchen was a duplicate of her mother's. She'd consider that later. For now she had to hide. She put her hands to her head to try to think what to do. She didn't have much time.

The root cellar! Was it possible that Jasper had a cellar too? She dropped to the floor in front of the stove, pushed aside the rug there, and felt with her hands. Yes, there was a latch! She pulled the door up and scrambled into the opening, not caring if there were a ladder or not, but there was. Her foot caught hold of it and she quickly and quietly lowered the hatch door and held on to the rope with all the force she could bear.

The sounds were muffled now, but she heard the door open. Someone was in the house. Was it Jasper or was it the man chasing her? Footsteps. She could hear them, but they were not moving about like someone who knew his way. They were stealthy, seeking footsteps.

She wondered if the door to the cellar was obvious. It had never occurred to her to ask her mother about it. Whenever she went down the cellar steps to get jams or pickles or potatoes or other canned goods, she just went. She made herself think about what the door felt like on the floor. It had an edge around it that would make it obvious, but her mother had a braided rug in front of the stove that hid the door. Then with a sinking heart she remembered the rug she had just pushed aside. The man was going to see it and he was going to know she was down here and he was going to find her.

She could hear him in the kitchen now. A quick walk around would tell him that no one was there. She prayed he wouldn't look down and see the rumpled rug. Then she heard him step quickly to the window. He grunted something and hurried toward the door. She held her breath.

Then she heard Jasper's voice.

No! Don't come to the house, Jasper! She screamed the words silently but she dare not make her presence known. Not yet. She strained to hear what was being said. Then the men came inside.

"I called out, but didn't seem like anyone was home." It was the voice of the man from the school yard.

"I was down at the barn. So, what can I do for you? Say, didn't I see you at the wedding? You must be new in town. Name's Ole Jasperson."

No, Jasper, don't be friendly! Get rid of him.

"Uh, yeah. I was wondering if you'd seen my dog. Went missing."

"Your dog? Is that what the rope is for? What's he look like? I'd be glad to help you find him. Care for some coffee?"

It sounded like Jasper turned from the man.

"No, I don't want coffee."

Melody's head shot up as the man's tone changed.

Jasper's voice changed too. "There's no need to pull a gun on me, mister. You want something, help yourself. I don't have much to steal."

A gun! Oh, Jasper!

Jasper held his hands out away from his sides as he sized up the man pointing a gun at him. The man wasn't very tall, but he had meaty arms and hands and a girth that wasn't made of fat but of muscle. Jasper had no idea what the man wanted, but he could see the coldness in his eyes and knew he wasn't someone to be trifled with. Jasper knew he had to be careful.

"Where is she?"

She? The question put Jasper off balance. "Who? Your dog?"

"Don't get smart. Where's that girl? I saw her run in here."

Jasper's expression didn't change, but his thoughts were in turmoil. *Is he talking about Melody? He has to be. But why?* Why was he after her and why would she be in his house?

"I live alone, fellow. There's no one here."

"We'll see about that." The man motioned with his gun for Jasper to move toward the next room. Jasper walked past the stove where he had been about to prepare coffee and inconspicuously straightened the rug with his foot.

Are you down there, Melody? "Lord, protect her. Send help!"

The man pressed the gun into Jasper's back and prodded him into the living area. He took a quick look around, not seeing any place to hide. "What's up there?" He motioned with his head to the staircase.

"My bedroom."

"You up there, girl?" The man called.

"I told you, there's no one—"

Jasper's words were cut short when the man hit him on the side of the head with the butt of his pistol. Stars danced before his eyes and he put his hand to his head and pulled it away, sticky with blood.

"Come out, girl, or I'll hit him again. He's already bleeding."

Don't, Melody! Jasper prayed Melody would stay put. If he could just convince the man she wasn't there, maybe she would have a chance to get away.

"If…if you saw someone around here, it could be…she went to my barn." Jasper forced the words out in a louder than normal voice, hoping Melody would hear and not move from her hiding place.

"No, she came in here. I saw her from the road." He raised his pistol again as if to strike Jasper. "Don't play games with me."

"You saw from the road? There's a back door. If someone ran in the door you saw, they could easily run out the back."

The man appeared to be considering this. He motioned Jasper back toward the kitchen. Once they rounded the wall separating the kitchen from the table, he saw the back door. The man looked at it and then at Jasper.

"Okay, so maybe she did run out there. I'll have to look for her after I take care of you." He uncoiled the rope with one hand while he kept the gun steady on Jasper. When the rope hit the floor, he glanced down.

"What do we have here?" He pushed at the rug in front of the stove with the toe of his boot. Jasper inwardly groaned as a corner of the cellar door became visible. The man looked back at Jasper. "You knew she was there the whole time, didn't you?"

eleven

Garrett was elated. He had a fortune! He had no idea how much, but according to the lawyer, it was considerable. All he had to do now was wait for the paperwork to be verified then the lawyer's firm would let him know the amount and he could decide if he wanted to keep it there in Chicago or have it transferred somewhere else. There was even mention of a house and whether he would keep it or sell it.

He couldn't contain his excitement. All the years of barely eking out a living and now this. If only his mother had lived to see it.

That thought stopped Garrett's excitement. But his mother did know about it. She ran from it. He frowned.

Jake and Mina had been quiet after the Wheatlys left. Garrett wondered if they were uncomfortable about him having money now. Would they expect some of it? He would be willing to give them some, providing there was enough, but he had to know how much he had first.

He had been pacing in the study where the others had left him to give him time to be alone. He looked down at the packet still unopened on Jake's desk. He was a little fearful to open it and see what it was his mother wanted him to know. Would it take away the euphoria he was feeling?

He sat down and reached for the packet. The seal crumbled as he twisted it open. As he expected there were only papers inside, and immediately he recognized his mother's handwriting.

Unbidden tears came to his eyes. She had known so much but still hadn't entrusted the information to him even though he were no longer a child. He pulled the papers forward and blinked the tears away as he began to read.

> *Dearest Garrett,*
>
> *Son, if you are reading this, it means I am gone. I am so sorry to leave you with the burden I have carried for so many years. I have lied to you.*
>
> *Your father was not a man named Gavin Foxe as I have told you. There was no such man. Your father was a man named Thorpe Prescott. You will*

remember we stopped in that little town in Minnesota to see his grave.

I met Thorpe when I was seventeen. He was a handsome man, so tall and good looking. I was a plain girl, had never been courted, and was swept off my feet by the attentions he heaped on me. I fell in love. My father refused to give me permission to marry Thorpe, but I disobeyed him and ran off and we were married. Soon after, I received word that my father had cut me off. I was no longer welcome in his home and I would inherit none of his money. That is when Thorpe left me. You see, he never loved me; he only wanted my father's money.

I was heartbroken, alone, and expecting you by this time. I soon heard things about your father— terrible things that made me fear him. I worried that if he knew I was going to have a baby, he might use you to somehow get my family's wealth through you. I changed my name and I kept out of sight, but still stayed where I could be near in case Thorpe changed. Love makes you think people will change, but Thorpe never did. The more I heard of his actions, the more I kept you hidden from him. Then one day news came that he was dead and that his body was in Minnesota.

I felt I had to know for sure. That's why I took you to that little town of Ulen so long ago. I had to see the grave for myself. Only then did I feel free of Thorpe Prescott and felt that you were no longer in danger from him.

As you know, we went back to Chicago and were welcomed by my dear friend. She told me my mother had died, and she knew my father was still looking for us, so she kept us with her until sadly she passed away. It's been a hard life for you, my son. For that, I'm sorry.

I don't have much longer to live. For some time now I have kept my sickness from you, but the doctor says there is no hope. When I am gone, you will be given this letter. I beg of you to wait until the lawyers inform you of your grandfather's death before you seek out information about him. I do not want him to control your life like he tried to control mine.

Do not expect anything from my father. I doubt he ever changed his mind about me, and I fear he would exact the punishment on you that he wished he could have given me for marrying Thorpe.

However, if by chance my father had a change of heart and you do inherit something, I have papers at the office of Wilson & Krause in Chicago that will give you full claim to whatever may be left to inherit. They are in your true name—Garrett Foxe Prescott. But, son, do not let money change who you are. I raised you the best I could, and even though we were poor, we were happy together.

I love you. May you have a good life.
Mother

Garrett folded the letter and wiped at his eyes. All the scrimping to get by, and there was money her father could have given them. Anger welled up inside him. Well, that money was going to be his now. No more working like a slave and being scorned by uppity young lawyers. He'd go back to Chicago and show them.

He stared with unseeing eyes out the window as dusk settled in. The Rodwells had been good to him, welcoming him in when he had nothing. They better not be expecting something in return now that he had means.

As soon as he had that thought, he was ashamed. Jake and Mina weren't like that. Garrett had known many people who only lived for what they could get, and he had not witnessed any self-centeredness in this family. If anything, he had to find a way to repay them without offending them. Maybe he could pay off the loan on their tractor or give some money to their church.

Maybe he could repay the Wheatlys for what his father had done to them in some way. He didn't wish to be selfish and uncaring like his grandfather.

And Harmony. He'd be able to treat her like a queen.

Of course, he had to know how much he was worth first. He gathered the papers together and left the study. The others were in the kitchen preparing the evening meal. They were quiet as Garrett entered the room, and that was another thing he appreciated about them. They didn't encroach on his personal business.

"You doing okay, Garrett?" Mina came to him and put an arm around his waist. He looked down at his pretty aunt.

"I am still in shock to find out that I had a rich grandfather." He took a chair. "My mother's letter to me cleared up some of the questions I've had." He told them about how Thorpe had wooed his mother into marrying him in order to get to her father's wealth. "When that failed, Thorpe left her. She changed her name and never told him about me in case he tried to use me to get it."

"I thought it might be something like that," Jake commented. "It's a hard thing to learn. You've never had a father's love, and you've certainly been shown how cruel a father can be as your grandfather was to your mother, but Garrett, there is a Father who loves you dearly. He loved you so much he sent his only son to die for you. There's a verse in Romans that says, 'But God commendeth his love toward us, in that, while we were yet sinners, Christ died for us.' You can experience that love and forgiveness if you place your faith in that simple message."

Garrett grew uncomfortable as Jake continued.

"I know you think Thorpe wasn't good enough to go to heaven, and you're absolutely right. He was not. But he's there, and you don't understand how we believe he's there. Think about it, Garrett. If your goodness merited you a place in heaven, then why would Jesus Christ have died for your sins on the cross? On what measuring scale would you claim that you had enough goodness? If you allow God to be the judge of that, he's already found you wanting. The Bible says, 'There is not a just man upon earth that doeth good and sinneth not.' And again in Romans it says, 'For all have sinned and come short of the glory of God.'

"If you say Thorpe was too evil to be allowed into heaven, I would have to ask you by what scale you judge Christ's atonement for sin. Was the death of Jesus Christ not enough to forgive Thorpe? Could a man commit more sin than God could cover? In Colossians 2:13 it says, '…having forgiven you all trespasses.' All means all."

Jake paused. "We're happy for you that you have an inheritance, but we would be even happier to know that you have become a child of God and will inherit all that he has to offer you in the heavenly places. Earthly riches cannot be taken with you when you die. Your grandfather and mother are evidence of that, but the riches of a life in Christ are eternal."

Garrett said nothing. He could see Mina nodding her head as Jake spoke and he saw Naomi smiling in encouragement as if she could coax him into accepting what Jake was saying. Josiah and Aaron were quiet, and Garrett wondered if they were praying. It almost made him angry the way they were ganging up on him. He was about to speak when the door burst open and Tobias rushed in.

"Is Melody here?"

"Melody? No. Why, has something happened?" Jake stood to his feet.

"She never came home from school. We've looked everywhere and we've been calling her name. We're worried because Grandpa stopped by to warn us that some animals have been spotted that have rabies. Melody wouldn't be able to see an animal acting strangely like that."

"We'll come now and help you look. Have you checked at Jasper's?"

"Yes, we went there right away, but no one was home, which is odd too. Jasper's horse is still there and so is his wagon."

"Did you go in the house?"

"We went in the front door and called and called."

"Josiah, get the horses."

Garrett touched Jake's arm. "How can I help?"

Jake hesitated. He looked between Garrett and Mina. "I don't know why, but I think there's something more here than Melody getting lost. Melody never gets lost, and had there been an animal attack, she would have called out. Either Jasper or Keane would have heard. There's always someone close by Melody, whether she's aware of it or not. Garrett, I want you to stay here and protect Mina and Naomi. Check around the place for anything suspicious. Something definitely is not right."

Mina took Jake's arm. "Be careful, dear. We'll be praying."

He gave her a quick kiss, smiled reassuringly at Naomi and left with the others. Garrett nodded at the women then headed out the door to scout around the house as Jake said. He heard Mina's voice behind him begin to pray.

All thought of his inheritance and his mother's letter were out of his mind as he made his way around the house and stood in the shadows while the other men rode off. He

tried to see through the settling gloom across the fields for any sign of her.
Melody, where are you?

twelve

Melody heard everything that went on while Jasper faced the man with the gun. She knew that Jasper had figured out where she was and was trying to lure the man outdoors. She was waiting for them to leave so she could make a break for help when she heard the man's exclamation of "What do we have here!" Then there was a lot of grunting and thuds as feet hit the floor above her head. A moment later there was silence except for someone's labored breathing.

Melody waited. There was something happening up there, someone moving about. She kept the rope for the cellar door firmly in her hands. If Jasper tried the door, she knew he would say something to her. If it was the other man, she was bound and determined not to let him get the door open.

But she was no match for him. He pulled her and the rope both up when he swung back the door. Her knees hit the ladder and the breath was nearly knocked out of her as she was pulled upward. She tried to climb out and scramble away, but the man grabbed the back of her jacket collar.

"I knew you were in the house! You should have come out, girl. Now, see what you've done!" He yanked her around to face something and she could only guess that it was Jasper.

"Jasper? Jasper!"

"He can't hear you. Wasn't too smart of him to try to take my gun." He gave Melody a shove. "Grab that rope hanging on the wall there. I'm tying you up next."

Does that mean that Jasper is tied up? If so, he must be alive. "Oh, please, God! Please let him be alive!"

The shove caused Melody to fall forward onto her knees. She felt around her for Jasper and her hand caught hold of his pant leg. She scrambled toward him. "Jasper! Are you all right?"

"Get away from him, and do what you're told. Get the rope."

Melody ignored the man and felt along Jasper's legs until she came to the ropes tying his ankles. Her hands moved up his arms and she realized his hands were tied behind his back. She was getting frantic. *Jasper! Jasper, my love, no!* She was reaching for his head and just felt the wetness on his scalp when she was roughly pulled away.

"I told you to get that rope!" The click of a hammer being pulled back on a pistol sounded like the gun had actually gone off in her ear, making Melody jump. The man pulled her to her feet.
"Get it!"

She was trembling as she put her arm out and started in the direction she thought she was supposed to go. Her hand touched something and she patted it until she realized it was Jasper's coat hanging on a hook. She felt with her hand to the right of it, but there was nothing. She was about to check the other side when the man grabbed her collar at the back of her neck again.

"What's the matter with you? Can't you see it? Now give it to me!"

She swung her hand until it connected with the rough loop of rope. She grabbed it and turned toward the man.

There was silence while she held the rope out. Then his voice came from the other side of her and she was twisted around to face him. She felt his hand wave back and forth in front of her face. "You're blind. You're blind as a bat." The words were spoken in disgust. The man swore. "If I'd a known that, I wouldn't have gone after you. You can't identify me. But now…"

Melody felt the rope taken from her.

"Turn around." In quick order he tied her hands and then her feet, just as Jasper was tied. She tried to pull away when a cloth went over her mouth, but he forced her head still while he tied the gag on her. "You could still yell." His explanation was almost apologetic. "And I can't have anyone finding you two until I get back. I'd take care of you now, but...I gotta make it look like an accident."

The words sent a chill down her back. *He's going to kill us too. He has to know that Jasper's seen him. "Please, Lord, not now. Not Jasper! I love him so."* It took her a moment to understand what she had just prayed. She loved this man who could even now be dying at her feet.

In the distance a bell was faintly clanging. Melody knew her family was looking for her and signaling for her to find the house. The man straightened from tying the rope as if he were listening. It seemed to spur him to move quicker.

The next sound Melody heard was Jasper being dragged along the floor and then a thud as he was deposited on the dirt floor of the root cellar. She felt the man's hands reach for her and she tried to wriggle away, but he picked her up and with more gentleness than she expected, he dropped her on top of Jasper. She heard the cellar door above her close.

With difficulty she rolled onto her side off Jasper and desperately hoped he wasn't badly injured from being dropped. She listened carefully and thought the man had left, but footsteps returned. She jumped when something pounded on the door then she realized to her horror that the man was putting nails in the sides of the hatch door to keep her or Jasper from pushing it open. Then the footsteps left and the house was quiet.

Dad and the boys will be looking for me. Melody tried to calm the panic building in her. There was no time to waste. She and Jasper had to get out and stop the man from killing Garrett. She struggled to get her bound hands under her. There was little space to move on the dirt floor, especially with Jasper out cold beside her. She was just thankful she could tell he was alive by his breathing. Once she was able to wiggle her hands around her legs and feet and got them in front of her, she reached down to her ankles and with her bound hands began poking the tips of her fingers into the ropes there trying to release the knots. She heard Jasper's muffled groan beside her. His mouth was gagged too.

All she could do was make some noises from behind her gag to let Jasper know she was there. She felt him move as if he were trying to sit up, but there was little room and his head banged into her. She felt the weight of his head on her shoulder and she leaned her head on his. For just a moment it was as if they embraced. Then he pushed his head against her harder and she understood that he wanted her to try to untie the cloth around his head. She pulled her hands away from the ropes on her ankles and went to work on the knot at the back of Jasper's head. She could only barely get her fingertips loose enough to grasp the cloth and she knew she was pulling on his hair, but she kept at it until finally it loosened and she felt Jasper swing his head from side to side and spit at the cloth in his mouth until he was freed of it.

"Melody!" His voice was frantic. "Are you all right? Did he hurt you?"

"Mmm, mmm! Mmm, mmm!" She hoped he understood that she was okay.

"Here, turn your head so I can get at those knots with my teeth." Melody turned and felt her hair being tugged and pulled as the cloth was wriggled free of her mouth. She turned back to speak to Jasper and bumped into his face. Without hesitation he kissed her, then kissed her cheeks and her eyes and laid his forehead against hers.

"If anything had happened to you…"

Melody couldn't speak. This was Jasper! But this wasn't the Jasper she knew, the old friend, the bachelor neighbor. This was the man she loved, whom she had loved for a long time without even knowing it.

Jasper was moving again. "I have to get you out of here. He could come back at any time."

"I can move my fingers some. Let me try those ropes on your hands." While Melody worked on the knots, she told Jasper all she knew about the two men and what the man had said before leaving them. "And he nailed the cellar door shut, Jasper. We won't be able to push it open."

"We'll try. Don't worry, sweetheart. We'll get free."

She smiled at the endearment. "How is your head?"

"Hurts like the dickens!" Jasper chuckled, surprising Melody. "But I'd go through it all again if it meant I could finally tell you that I love you." He spoke over his shoulder as Melody continued to tug at the knots on his wrists. "I love you, Melody Wheatly. I've loved you for a very, very, very long time. Do you mind?"

"Oh, Jasper! You do beat all! You picked a fine time to tell me! But I'm glad. I'm glad you did because when you were unconscious and I thought you might be dead, I knew how much you meant to me. I love you too."

Despite their circumstances, Jasper laughed again. "As soon as I get your dad's permission, I'm marrying you, girl."

The ropes began to pull free and soon Jasper was freeing Melody's hands. "You really want a blind wife? Are you sure?"

"I've been waiting for you to finally *see* me, you little blind fool." He hugged her quickly then began to work on the ropes at his feet while Melody undid hers. "You've been blind in more ways than one, my sweet."

"Jasper!"

"What?" He turned to her even though in the dark he could see nothing.

"Your kitchen! Is that why your kitchen is just like my mother's? You did that for me?"

"You weren't supposed to know about that until you fell in love with me, but under the circumstances, yes. I designed the whole house so that you would know your way around just like you do now. Is that okay? I know how much you want to feel independent and all, so if you want to make changes that would be more to your liking, I'll do it."

"Oh, Jasper! What did I ever do to deserve you?"

"You've got that wrong." They were free of the ropes now and Jasper pulled Melody to her feet. "I don't deserve you." His arms went around her. "I bought this land near your family so that you could be close to them. I know you worry about your parents taking care of you, but I hope that even after I'm gone someday, you'll have our children to watch out for you."

"Children? Are you sure, Jasper? I am blind, you know."

"There's nothing you can't do, my dear Melody. But first, we have to get out of here if we hope to have that life together, Lord willing." Melody heard Jasper climb the ladder and grunt as he pushed against the door. Suddenly she tugged on his pant leg.

"Jasper! I hear someone."

He stepped down and held her while together they listened. Was the man back already? But this time there were many footsteps and then voices calling out their names.

"We're down here! We're here!" They shouted as loudly as they could.

"Jasper? Melody?"

Melody clung to Jasper in relief as Jasper responded to her father's call. "It's nailed shut, Keane. Hurry!"

In no time the men had the door opened and Jasper helped Melody up the ladder into her father's arms. She wept in relief, but turned back to Jasper when her father exclaimed, "What happened? You're bleeding all over the place."

"Jasper?" Melody held onto her father's arm while she reached for Jasper. He came to her side and she stepped into his embrace. "You're hurt bad, aren't you!"

"Oh, it doesn't look too bad." The happiness in Keane's voice made Melody turn in question to her father again. "Looks to me like he's feeling pretty good right now. About time you two found each other."

"Oh, Dad!" Melody knew she was blushing.

"Jake, Garrett's in danger." Quickly Jasper related Melody's story and then what had happened at his house.

"He said it has to look like an accident." Melody added.

Jake yelled over his shoulder as he ran to the door. "We left Garrett guarding the house with Mina and Naomi!"

thirteen

It was getting harder to see with no moonlight to illumine the night. Garrett peered into the blackness, trying to make out the shapes of the buildings on the farm. He couldn't. It made him understand in a small way what it was like for Melody with her blindness. Yet, she always seemed so confident in her steps and movements and seemed to resent being offered help. He supposed it was because she really was in control and didn't like to have to rely on others. Was she in trouble now?

Jake's words in the kitchen came back to him. Why did they all feel the need to preach to him? Was it because they thought that deep down he was like his father and needed spiritual help? He was nothing like his father. They should see that by now.

It was Melody's words that haunted him the most. *"I was blind, but now I see."* Was he blind? He wanted to see what they were telling him, but he couldn't understand why it was so important. He remembered that Melody also said, *"It really is a matter of life and death. Will you spend eternity in heaven or hell?"*

A snapping branch made Garrett jump, and he swung around to the noise but could see nothing. Then a shape moved. Garrett didn't move, didn't breathe, didn't even blink. A man was inching his way along the back of the house. The only reason Garrett could see him was because the light from inside the window was just enough for him to make out his form. Who was he? Why was he sneaking around the Rodwell farm?

Garrett had no weapon with him, but as the man moved along, Garrett could see that he carried a pistol. His heart began to thump. What could he do? He had to protect Mina and Naomi, no matter what.

Then he remembered the axe by the woodpile behind him. He started slowly backing up, feeling the ground with each step before he put his weight down. The fallen leaves were damp on the ground and made no crackling noise as he moved farther and farther away from the man, yet keeping him in sight the whole time. Once the man turned his way, but Garrett stopped and stood like a statue. Could he see him? The man raised himself up to peek into one of the windows and Garrett took that opportunity to bend down in search of the axe. His hand bumped the handle and the axe began to fall forward, but Garrett grasped it on its way to the ground. He raised it in his hand just as he heard the crash of the man coming toward him. The man was no longer visible, but Garrett swung the axe in his general direction and made contact with the side of the man's head with the broadside of the axe.

The man grunted in pain but didn't stop coming. Garrett swung again, but this time he missed and the man tackled him to the ground. Garrett lost the axe in the struggle and found himself being overpowered by the sheer weight and muscle of the man who punched and slugged him. He didn't know if any of his return blows had any effect on the brute or not, but he kept on punching. They must have been making a great deal of noise because the door of the house swung open and suddenly there was Mina holding a rifle in her hands aimed right at them, Naomi beside her with a lantern in her hands.

"Get away from Garrett, mister, or I'll shoot!"

The man continued to beat Garrett with his fists as if he didn't hear her. "Get back in the house, Mina!" Garrett yelled.

The rifle went off and Garrett heard the whistle of the bullet above their heads. That stopped the man, but only for a moment. He reached for his pistol and aimed it at Mina.

"No!" Garrett dove for the man's gun just as it went off. Almost simultaneously the rifle fired again and Garrett saw the man drop to the ground. He tried to get up to go to him and get the weapon from him, but he couldn't seem to make himself stand. He pulled himself up on one elbow and tried to push his body off the ground with his other arm, but it wasn't working. He slumped back down.

"Garrett!" Mina was beside him.

"Get…his…gun…" Garrett managed to get the words out. Then he knew nothing more.

"That was a shot!" Jake urged his horse to go faster down the driveway to his home, the men behind him. He pulled his rifle from the scabbard by the saddle, fear for his wife and daughter utmost in his mind. Cries for Divine help came from within him as he swung his leg over the horse and ran to the house. He could see Naomi on the front porch holding a lantern in the air. He looked to where she was pointing and barely understood what she was yelling to him as he searched for Mina.

There she was, crouched on the ground over a body. As he ran to her he saw another body behind her.

"Mina, are you all right?" He reached for her as she stood and flung herself into his arms.

"It's Garrett, Jake! He's been shot. The man was trying to shoot me, but Garrett jumped in front of him to protect me."

"Are *you* hurt?" Jake couldn't let go of his wife.

"No. But…"

"What? What's wrong?" He tried to look into her face for an answer as the others came up behind them.

"I shot that man over there. I think I killed him." Mina's voice was shaking.

Keane stepped past Jake and Mina and bent down by the stranger. "He's still breathing." He picked up the pistol not far from the man's hand then turned to look at Garrett. "Bring the lantern, someone."

In the glow of the lantern Keane looked over Garrett's wounds. "It's high up on his chest. We better get him inside now and go for the doctor."

"I'll go." Josiah got a nod from his father.

"Get the sheriff too."

Jake handed Mina over to Naomi who led her into the house then he and Keane with the help of Aslak and Tobias carried Garrett into the house and put him in Jake and Mina's room. Aaron stood guard over the other man in case he came to, and relinquished his guard duty when his father returned.

"What do we do with this one?"

Jake checked his wound. "Mina got him on the shoulder bone, probably cracked it. I'll bandage it up until the doc and sheriff get here. Let's get him into the barn and make sure he doesn't get away. I want some answers to all this."

A rider came at a gallop down the driveway and Keane got behind a tree with his rifle ready. But it was Jasper who called out.

Keane stepped from behind the tree. "Thought you were told to stay with the women and get that head bandaged up."

"It's bandaged and those women would have come here themselves if I hadn't. They're worried sick about all the gunfire, and they're not the only ones. What's happened?"

Keane motioned for Jasper to follow him to the barn. Aslak was there, holding a shotgun on their prisoner while Jake tied him to a post. "This the fellow who put that gash in your head?"

Jasper knelt down and turned the man's face to the light. "Yeah. It's him."

Keane spoke to Aslak. "I need you to go back to our house and tell the women what's happened so that they aren't worried." As Aslak started for the door, Keane stopped him with a hand on his arm. "Be careful what you say about Garrett. Just tell the truth; we don't know for sure how bad it is." Aslak nodded.

"Garrett's been shot? Melody said the man was told to make it look like an accident. What happened?"

Keane and Jake filled Jasper in as they went to the house. Mina was back at the stove heating water in case the doctor would need it and she had coffee on and sandwiches ready for the men.

"Mina, what are you doing? We don't need food. Come sit down, dear." Jake coaxed his wife to a chair.

"I have to keep busy. My hands are just shaking. Did they tell you I shot that man?" she asked Jasper.

"*You* shot him?"

The whole story was told again by Jake as Keane went in to check on Garrett. When he returned his face was somber.

"He's still out. Other than stopping the bleeding and keeping him warm, I don't know what else we should do until the doctor comes."

"I do." Jake said. They bowed their heads with him as he called upon the Lord, first thanking him not only for the safety of his family but also of Jasper and Melody, then praying for Garrett. "As far as we know, he still hasn't seen his need of you, Lord."

They waited then. Jasper relayed the account of Melody's encounter with the men at the schoolhouse and what happened when she tried to hide at his house. Mina was still shaking and getting up every few minutes to tend to something in the kitchen, so Jasper decided to try to take her mind off the night's troubles.

"I have some news."

The men turned to him with grins on their faces, knowing what he wanted to say, but Mina kept working.

"Mina? Mina, I said I have some news."

"Oh, you do, Jasper. What is it? Please, not something else horrible."

"No, I don't think so. Melody is going to marry me."

Naomi jumped to her feet and twirled around the room, her hand covering her mouth to keep from making a noise that would bother the wounded man in the next room, but Mina never turned around. "That's nice, dear." She said from the kitchen.

The men grinned at one another. Suddenly Mina's head popped around the corner and she frowned at Jasper.

"What did you say?"

"I said Melody is going to marry me."

Mina rushed to Jasper, and he got to his feet just as she threw her arms around him. "Well, it's about time you told her how you felt about her, Ole Jasperson! We've all been wondering for years how much longer it was going to take. You've been making googly eyes at her since she was sixteen."

Jasper was stunned as he studied the faces one by one in front of him. "Seriously? You all knew?"

"Of course we knew. You'd have to be blind—oh, my goodness! That wasn't the right thing to say!"

The laughter that followed Mina's embarrassment was a good relief for all of them. It wasn't long after that they heard the approach of horses and knew the doctor was on his way. Keane led the sheriff to the barn and explained the evening's happenings, while Mina took the doctor in to see Garrett. They all waited in the kitchen until he came out, his face grim.

"I don't like where I see the bullet lodged, but I've got to get it out of there because there's bound to be internal bleeding. We're going to have to do surgery here. We can't move him. You up to it, Mrs. Rodwell?"

"Yes, of course. Water's hot, doctor."

Jake stood. "Is he awake? I'd like to talk to him."

"He's been mumbling a bit. You can go in, but don't tire him out. He's going to need his strength if he's going to recover." The doctor took the coffee Mina handed him and sat down by Jasper, looking with interest at the bandage on his head. "I think I might as well take a look at that while I'm here."

Jake entered his bedroom and quietly approached the bed. Garrett's face was white and his eyes closed. Jake prayed silently while he watched the man and was relieved when Garrett opened his eyes and looked at him. Garrett tried to speak, but Jake hushed him.

"Don't try to talk, Garrett. Mina and Naomi are fine, they never got hurt. I can't thank you enough for protecting them like you did."

Garrett visibly relaxed and Jake knew he had been worried.

"We got the man who was after you, and the sheriff will take care of him now. Okay?"

Garrett gave a slight nod of his head.

"You're going to have to have surgery to have that bullet out. The doctor's getting ready. We're all praying for a good recovery from this. You just get the rest you need now." Jake turned to leave, but he felt Garrett reach for his hand. He looked back at the young man and saw fear in his eyes. He hesitated, not knowing if this was the right time to bring up Garrett's need of Christ, but he saw something in Garrett's eyes that told him it was.

"Jesus died for your sins, Garrett. He died, he was buried, and he rose from the dead. You believe he did that for you, and you're saved. It's as simple as that. You can be cleansed and forgiven and be assured of heaven all at the same time. You don't deserve it, nor do I, but it's ours because of God's love and grace toward us. I can't do it for you. Just believe it, Garrett." He squeezed the hand in his and was rewarded with a bit of movement of Garrett's head and a curve on his lips. Jake had to lean closer to hear Garrett's words as his mouth moved.

"I…do."

"Praise God!"

"If you please, Mr. Rodwell, we have work to do here." The doctor came in followed by Mina. Jake's smile at his wife told her what had happened and she nodded and smiled back then turned to assist the doctor. Jake quietly left the room and went to tell the others.

He was not surprised to see Tuva and Melody in the kitchen.

"We had to come, Jake. I've sent Aslak to get Harmony too. She'll want to be here." Tuva explained. "I'll go help now."

"Wait." Jake quickly told the group about Garrett's decision. There were tears of joy and then Jake led them in prayer for the doctor and for the life of the young man in the next room.

"What needs to be done in the kitchen?" Melody asked Naomi.

"I think we just need to keep coffee on. Mom has been making so many sandwiches that I don't think we can eat them all."

Aslak and Harmony arrived an hour later. Aslak, worn out from his night's rides fell asleep on the sofa, but Harmony went straight to Melody and slipped her hand in her sister's. Garrett's news was shared again and Harmony cried on Melody's shoulder.

"Is he going to die, Melody? Tell me the truth." She whispered in Melody's ear.

Melody could hear the fear in her voice. "The doctor is going to do all he can. We have to leave it in God's hands.

It was a long night's vigil. They talked off and on and were silent other times. Melody rested her head on Jasper's shoulder and thought how right it felt to be there. She was happy. Despite all the trouble they had been through and the tenseness of waiting for news about Garrett, she was happy. Jasper's even breathing told her he was asleep, and though she was tired, sleep was far from her.

It humbled her to discover that Jasper had loved her for so long when she only just learned of her love for him. Would she be able now to see him as her future husband rather than just as the friend and joking companion he had been? She knew she would. Jasper was now both friend and the love of her life. The fear of being dependent was no longer there. She and Jasper would build a life together. They needed each other.

She felt Harmony stir beside her. She knew her sister cared for Garrett, possibly more than any of the other men whose attentions she had enjoyed, but was it real this time? And if it was, would the inheritance Garrett was to receive going to change that? Would it change him?

So many questions ran through Melody's mind. She could only give them to the Lord one by one and pray for wisdom as the events unfolded.

Everyone became alert when the doctor came into the room followed by Mina and Tuva. There was an audible sigh from the group, and Melody turned to Jasper for an explanation. Both he and Harmony said at the same time, "They're smiling."

Melody heard Harmony laugh softly as she leaned across her and spoke to Jasper. "I guess you'll be the one telling her these things now, Jasper."

"Gladly," was his response.

Melody felt Jasper squeeze her hand as they waited for the doctor to speak.

"It went well. The bullet is out and the bleeding stopped. Now he needs rest and water and when he's ready, some good soups to build up his strength. I'm sure you ladies can handle that."

"Thank you, Lord! Thank you, doctor!" Jake stood and reached to shake the doctor's hand, but the man held his hands up.

"I need to clean up first, Jake, and some breakfast would be good before I get back to my other patients."

Melody spoke quietly to Jake. "Is it morning already? I have to get to the school and so does Harmony."

Keane walked over to his daughters. "I'll send the boys to the schools to tell them you both will be absent today. I think we all need a day to recover."

Melody nodded and Harmony thanked her father. Just as Melody rose to go help in the kitchen she thought of something. "Dad!"

"What is it, Mel?"

"That man, the one in the buggy, the one you said was from Chicago, he said that he had Garrett sign papers that his money would go to another relative if he died."

"Yes? You heard the doctor. He's not going to die."

Jasper put his hand on Melody's elbow. "Go on."

"He said that he had a lady, an actress—what was her name?—who would say she is Garrett's sister and that she would get a share, he would get a share, and the man who's in the barn, he would get a share."

"But—"

"He thinks Garrett is already dead. He sent that man to kill Garrett tonight, to make it look like an accident. I think the man might have succeeded if he hadn't been side-tracked by Jasper and me. And didn't you say the lawyer was getting on last night's train, Jake? He's going to go back and steal Garrett's inheritance."

The room was silent.

"But what can we do?" Jake asked finally. "Should we telegram the law office about Garrett, saying he's still alive and that they shouldn't do anything yet?"

"I don't think a telegram would get to them if that dirty lawyer is working there. For all we know the whole place is crooked and is in on this plan to get rid of Garrett. Sheriff?" Jasper put the problem before the law man.

"You could be right, Jasper." Melody waited, wondering what the sheriff was thinking. "Maybe one or more of you need to go there and find out."

"What about your prisoner? Should he be there to point the finger at that Gladstone fellow?"

"No, I don't think he has to be there, but we should get a statement in writing from him. I'm pretty sure with all the charges against him that he'll be willing to cooperate to save his own skin. Now that it's daylight, I'll get him to town and get that taken care of. I might have to wake the judge." Melody heard the sheriff chuckle as if he wouldn't mind waking the man.

"Do we need something in writing from Garrett? He won't be up to that for a few days, I'm guessing, and if what you're saying is true, we need to get there now. Someone should leave today." Jake put his thoughts to the sheriff.

"Well, I'm not a lawyer, mind, but I'd say you should go, Jake, because you saw the lawyer here in your home, correct?"

Melody assumed Jake nodded.

"And you heard what he said and saw him push those papers on Garrett to sign, like you told me. Okay, so either you or your wife should go, but…"

Melody heard movement in the room as if everyone had turned toward her.

"I think Melody should also go because she's the one who heard the lawyer tell that guy in the barn to kill Garrett and make it look like an accident. Right, Melody?"

She nodded.

"And, from what you just said, Melody, you also heard him say he was going to have a lady pretend to be Garrett's sister. So that's another thing that you have an eyewitness account of."

"Eyewitness? Sheriff, I didn't *see* him. I only heard him."

"Of course. That should be enough. And you, Jasper, how much did you hear the guy say at your house?"

Jasper didn't answer immediately and Melody knew he was trying to remember. "Not much, actually. I was unconscious for most of it. I knew he was after Melody, but I didn't understand why."

"Then your testimony will only be good against your attacker, not the lawyer. No need for you to go to Chicago."

"If Melody's going, I'm going." Jasper declared, putting his arm around her.

"Well, just so she's one of the ones going." The sheriff stretched and Melody heard some cracking noises like he had moved his head from side to side. "Guess I better get things underway."

"Breakfast first, sheriff." Naomi surprised them all when with mature authority she herded the people into the dining area and started bringing food out that she had been busy preparing.

Melody put a hand out to stop Jasper from joining the others. "Jasper, if it's true that I have to be the one to go to Chicago, then..." She hesitated.

"What is it? Are you afraid? You know I'll be there beside you."

"That's just it. I don't think you should be. I...I don't know how to say this...look, Jasper, there are things that I need help with...you know I'm as independent as I can be, but...you see, my mother and Harmony help me with things..."

"Like...?"

"Well, like...we'll be gone overnight, right? So I'll need to sleep somewhere. Now, how could you help me find my way around in a strange...a strange bedroom?" Melody stumbled in embarrassment over the word.

Jasper gently brushed her hair away from her face. "We could get married first."

"What? No. I mean, yes, I want to marry you...very much, but no, I don't want to just get married quickly so you can help me find my way around...no!"

He chuckled. "Okay, I'll stop teasing you. I see your point. You need a woman along to help you with...for...things I couldn't do yet. But someday will." He promised in a low voice.

"Oh, Jasper. You do beat all."

Jasper just laughed. "But I can still go along. I don't want you going that far without me."

"Jasper. It's expensive. Maybe we should hear what the others think first."

It was decided that Jake and Mina would accompany Melody, and even though Jasper still protested that he should go too, Melody pressed reason on him. There was a flurry of activity as they packed and got ready to leave on the afternoon train. The sooner they could get there, the better, the sheriff told them. Keane and Tuva would take care of both farms, and would stay at the Rodwells so that Tuva could watch over Garrett. Jasper would help out wherever needed.

Melody was weary as she and Harmony worked together to put her clothing bag together. It wasn't until Harmony helped her change out of the brown skirt and jacket she had been wearing the day before that bruises were discovered all down Melody's side.

"Oh, my goodness, Melody! That must be painful." Harmony exclaimed in horror at the bruises.

"I haven't even felt them yet, but I'm stiff. I guess I haven't had time to notice."

Harmony started arranging her sister's hair. "You and Jasper, huh? I wondered when you'd figure out that you loved him. He's been in love with you a long time."

Melody spun around on the chair. "How do you know that? You flirted with him all the time. I thought you were interested."

Harmony shrugged and turned Melody away from her again so she could finish braiding her hair. "I only did it to try to make Josiah jealous. Jasper only had eyes for you!"

"But it's not Josiah you want anymore, is it?"

Harmony sighed. "I really like Garrett," she admitted. "But I was afraid to let my feelings for him grow because he wasn't saved and didn't seem interested in the Lord. You know how important that is to me, to us. Now I have mixed feelings. I'm so happy he's accepted Jesus, but he's about to inherit a bucket full of money. He'll probably move back to Chicago and won't want anything to do with a farm girl from Minnesota."

Melody laughed. "You don't know that. You may be surprised. But whatever happens, just keep trusting the Lord for your future and seek his will. I've learned that God wants the best for us, and just when I thought I was resigned to a life of being alone, he provided me with a friend who loves me and wants to marry me." Melody yawned. "Pray for me on this trip, Harmony. It is a bit frightening to go to any unfamiliar place, but a city! I'm glad Mina will be there. And watch out for Jasper too, will you?"

Harmony laughed. "You'll be back in no time and you two will start planning a wedding. I assume I get to stand up with you?"

"Of course." Melody stood and hugged her. "Only if I get to do the same at your wedding."

Chicago

It was the noise that struck Melody the most. Motor cars seemed to be everywhere, with their horns honking and people shouting for others to get out of their way. She could hear horses and the wheels turning on buggies, so she knew that the streets were crowded with both, the new pushing the old out of the way. There were so many people talking at once wherever they went that Melody could not make out what they were saying. It just seemed to be a steady hum.

A shrill whistle made her jump, and she felt Mina's hand on her arm steady her. How thankful she was for Mina! Melody had only traveled short distances on the train before, but this long ride and changing trains at stations and having to find the facilities were all strenuous for those who had sight to help them. For Melody it was bordering on terrifying. Just being served a meal was making her nervous. At home everything was in place and she knew that her food had been put on her plate in a certain order. She appreciated again that Mina quietly told her the location of the things before her and allowed her the dignity to eat in some sort of normalcy. It made her question if Jasper truly understood what responsibilities he was taking on in asking her to marry him.

To think she had considered leaving home to travel to a city and work in a school for the blind. She knew now that all she wanted was to be with Jasper, in her own home, near her own town, and by her family. At one time she had wondered if she was doing enough by staying in the world she was accustomed to, but now she felt at peace about it. She knew she was willing to go wherever the Lord could best use her, but she also knew that sometimes that place was right where she was. That unsettled feeling she had before was of her own making. She was finally learning to accept who she was and to be confident where she was.

"We should get to the lawyer's office right away," Jake said. "I'll go see what I can find for transportation there. You ladies wait right here where I can find you again, Lord willing."

Melody smiled as she heard the uneasiness in Jake's voice. She wasn't the only one who felt out of their element in this strange city. She jumped when she felt a tug on her sleeve.

"Got any spare change, miss?" The voice appeared to belong to a child.

"I...uh..."

"Here you go, young man. Poor little thing! Run off now." Mina shooed the boy away. She held on to Melody's arm as she explained. "There are always some young children around these stations begging for a coin or two. It was that way in Toledo where I was from, but be careful, Melody. They will grab your purse from you if you aren't watchful."

"But he sounded so young! Surely he wasn't a thief."

"Don't be fooled. The young here find out quickly how to survive and if that means stealing, they'll do it."

"But where are his parents? Why isn't he in school?"

"He's most likely an orphan. It could be he's never been to school. A lot of children work in the factories here under terrible conditions. Jake's coming now."

Melody held her bag close to her side, heeding Mina's warning. The city had become even more distasteful to her after hearing what Mina said. How could people live under these conditions? She wrinkled her nose as odors found their way to her. They passed by places that permeated an awful stench.

Jake found a cab, a buggy with a driver, and gave him the address for Wilson & Krause's office. Mina tried to describe what they were seeing as the cab winded its way through the streets. The late fall air was chilly and Melody was thankful for the rug that was placed over her lap for the journey. She listened carefully as Jake and Mina told about the tall buildings and fancy clothing of the people they passed.

"Oh, look at that! What is that, Jake?" Before Jake could answer Mina's question, she'd burst out with another. "I've never seen anything like that. Look! What do you suppose that's for?" Then she'd remember Melody and apologize and try to explain, only to exclaim about something else. Melody felt it was all a whirlwind to her.

The cab stopped finally and they got out. Melody heard Jake give the man some money and ask him how they could get a ride to a hotel when they finished their business. She and Mina waited quietly while the men discussed a few things.

"He's going to take our bags to the hotel and return for us in an hour's time." He told the women as the cabbie moved off.

"Oh, Jake! Can you trust him? He might just take off with our bags!" Mina exclaimed. Melody waited for Jake's answer, wondering if he thought he had made a mistake.

"We'll just have to trust that he doesn't. Here's the office. Let's get this taken care of first and we'll worry about the cab later." He led them forward.

Melody sensed right away that the offices of Wilson & Krause were something to behold. She heard Mina's quick intake of breath and wondered what she was seeing. Melody could smell the fragrance of flowers, and Mina whispered something about polished woodwork as they crossed a thickly carpeted floor and stopped.

"May I help you?" The voice was curt, almost condescending.

"We'd like to speak to the owner, please." Jake was polite.

"Mr. Wilson or Mr. Krause?"

"Which one is handling the Garrett Foxe Prescott case?" Jake asked.

There was a pause. "I'm sorry. I'm not at liberty to divulge that information. Do you have an appointment with either Mr. Wilson or Mr. Krause? No? Then I suggest you make an appointment." There was a rustling of papers. "We have an opening next week."

"No, that won't do. We need to speak to someone today, right now, in fact."

"I'm afraid that is impossible. Excuse me."

Melody heard a chair move. They had been dismissed, but Jake was not taking no for an answer.

"Come along, ladies."

Melody took Mina's arm and moved with her away from the woman they had been speaking to. She heard the woman's voice raised now as she came after them.

"Hold on! You can't just walk in there."

Melody followed Mina through a doorway and heard Jake saying, "Excuse me, are you Mr. Wilson?"

"What is the meaning of this? Miss Kris!"

"I'm sorry, Mr. Wilson. They just barged in."

"Sir, I'm here on the matter of Garrett Prescott and one of your employees, a man named Bill Gladstone."

Melody waited for a response from the man in the room. Finally he said, "It's okay, Miss Kris, I'll handle this. Shut the door, please." The door shut with a soft click. "Please, take a seat. Shall we start with introductions? As you have heard, I'm Bernard Wilson, senior partner of the firm. And you are?"

"Jacob Rodwell, sir. This is my wife Wilhelmina and my neighbor Melody Wheatly. Sir, we—"

"And what is your relationship to Mr. Prescott?"

"My wife is his aunt, a sister to his father. We—"

"Before we continue," Mr. Wilson interrupted. "I'd just like to say that on behalf of the firm of Wilson & Krause, we extend our sincere sympathy to you and your family—"

"He's not dead!" Mina burst out the words.

Melody could only wonder what the man's expression was after that pronouncement.

"What did you say?"

Jake spoke again. "We've been trying to tell you that Garrett Foxe—I mean, Garrett Prescott—is not dead though he is recovering from being shot, and we're here to tell you that the man you sent to Minnesota, Bill Gladstone, was heard plotting Garrett's murder with a man named Lee. Mr. Gladstone was also heard planning to have an actress named…"

Melody spoke up. "Lorna Landly."

"…named Lorna Landly to pretend to be Garrett's sister. The plan was for her to receive Garrett's inheritance from his grandfather to be split among the three of them, Bill Gladstone, Miss Landly, and Lee." Jake paused for a breath.

"Do you have proof of these malicious claims? Why is Mr. Prescott not here to speak for himself? Oh—you did say he had been shot."

Melody heard Jake pull papers from inside his coat. "This is a letter from the sheriff in our town explaining the whole thing. This one's a signed statement from Lee, confessing to his part in the plot and naming Bill Gladstone as the planner. This is from the doctor detailing the wound Garrett received at the hands of Lee, and this lady here…" He paused and Melody assumed he was pointing to her. "...Melody Wheatly heard the two men say clearly what they intended to do. It, too, is written in a statement signed by Miss Wheatly. I will also add that Miss Wheatly and her fiancé were attacked by this man named Lee, imprisoned, and threatened with death because of what she had witnessed."

There was silence as the man, apparently seated at a desk now, shuffled through the papers. By the length of time that passed, Melody guessed that he was carefully reading each one.

"If you want, you can verify who we are by asking Mr. Casper to come in. He was with Mr. Gladstone in our home, although he was not a part of this plot."

Mr. Wilson barely looked up and replied almost absently, "Mr. Casper left our employ immediately upon his return from Minnesota." Then he looked up. "You are sure that it was Bill Gladstone who said the things in this statement? You would swear to it in a court of law?"

Mina nudged Melody, and she understood that the man had been speaking to her. "Yes, sir. One thing you must know is that I am blind. I did not see either man, but I heard them. I can, without any doubt, verify it was Mr. Gladstone just by his voice. Both my...my fiancé and I have already identified Lee as the man who attacked us, but I am the only one who heard the plot between Mr. Gladstone and Lee."

Melody waited for a response.

"You're blind? I don't see how that would make you a credible witness."

"Sir, if I may." Jake stood. "My wife and I have seen Bill Gladstone when he came to our home to speak with Garrett. We were suspicious of him at the time because he pushed Garrett to sign papers, papers that said should he die, the inheritance would go to any other heirs who were found. Now, we didn't want Garrett to sign without taking time to read the document, but Mr. Gladstone rushed him through, having him sign several papers."

Jake stopped and Melody wondered why. She thought he had been leading up to something else, but Mr. Wilson had a comment.

"There was only one paper that we sent with Mr. Gladstone for Mr. Prescott to sign. It was the paper to accept the inheritance."

"Has Mr. Gladstone produced a woman, claiming to be a relative yet?" Mina asked.

"No. He should be back before long though." It appeared the man was thinking.

"What I was getting at, Mr. Wilson, is that even though Mr. Gladstone has seen my wife and I, he has never, to my knowledge, seen Miss Wheatly. If you want proof that she can identify him, I suggest you have him come into the office. Have several men come in. She'll be able to tell you which one he is."

"Your story is incredulous even though your papers appear to be in order. However, if you expect me to believe that this young woman is blind—"

"Ouch!" Melody was startled when something hit her in the face. Her hands flew up to rub the spot, and Mina jumped to her feet.

"That was the rudest thing I have ever seen anyone do!"

Mr. Wilson's voice was apologetic. "I am sorry. Please forgive me, Miss Wheatly, but I had to be sure you were telling the truth." Melody heard him step around the desk and pick up the item he had thrown at her.

"What was that?" She asked Mina.

"A small notebook. The nerve!" Mina was fuming.

Mr. Wilson's voice was closer now and he took Melody's hand. "I still can't believe that Bill Gladstone would betray the trust of this company, but I will agree to a little test if you are willing, my dear."

Melody nodded, but Mina was still upset with the man. "What kind of little test? Are you going to throw more things at her?"

"Mina." Jake tried to calm his wife.

"No, your wife has every right to her indignation. As a lawyer I've seen people try to defraud in so many ways it would make your head spin. I am a cautious man and I don't like to be made a fool of. If it's true what you say about Bill Gladstone, I will prosecute him myself! Now, here is my plan."

Melody waited on a soft leather chair in the corner of Mr. Wilson's office. She wasn't sure where Jake and Mina had been taken, but was told that they were comfortable and would be brought back in after the *test* was over. They had taken her coat and bag with them, and she now held a small notebook and a pencil in front of her. It seemed incongruous to her that she pretend to be a secretary, but that was Mr. Wilson's plan. He told no one else what he was doing, not even his own secretary Miss Kris.

"Here's your water, Miss Wheatly." She raised her hand and took the glass he offered. She tried not to make a face at the taste of the city water, but was thankful for something to quench her thirst. It had been a long day already and it still wasn't over.

"Are you ready?" Mr. Wilson put the question to her.

She held the glass out, not knowing where to set it until she felt him take it from her. "I think so. You just want me to pretend to take notes while you speak to the men and you want me to shake my head if it is not Mr. Gladstone and nod my head if it is, right?"

"Yes, that's right. Do you have any questions?"

"How will I know if you are looking at me?"

"Excuse me?"

"If I'm shaking or nodding my head, how will I know you've seen it?"

"Oh, I hadn't thought of that." He seemed to be rubbing at his chin as he thought and Melody wondered if he had whiskers. She was glad Jasper didn't. *Oh, Jasper! I miss you.* She forced herself to pay attention as Mr. Wilson spoke again. "I'll say, 'Very good!' How's that? I'll say it after I've seen your signal."

He almost seems to be enjoying himself. "Yes, sir."

"Okay. Let's begin." Melody nearly jumped when she heard a buzzer. "Miss Kris." She heard the secretary's voice speak as if she were on a telephone. "Yes, sir?" Mr. Wilson paused, then Melody heard him say, "Nothing, Miss Kris."

Melody frowned. *What now?*

Mr. Wilson chuckled. "I can't very well ask her to send someone in because I'd have to say their name. What kind of test would that be if I said, 'Send in Mr. Gladstone'? You see? Sorry, I...I mean, do you understand?"

Melody was growing tired of the unnecessary test and Mr. Wilson's condescending way with her. She stood. "It's obvious you still don't believe me. I think we'll just have to get a policeman here to make the arrest, and you can try to get your lawyer out of jail if you think he's not guilty. As you said, our paperwork is in order, and we're not about to let him get away with attempted murder."

"Now, you just hold on!"

There was a knock on the door and it opened.

"Mr. Wilson? Oh, excuse me, I didn't know you had a client."

Melody froze when she heard Bill Gladstone's voice.

"No, it's okay. Come in, come in. You have some news for me?"

Melody began nodding her head. She waited for Mr. Wilson to give her his signal that he saw her, but he didn't. She nodded again.

"Is there something wrong?" Bill's question was hesitant.

"No, this is a new girl just getting used to the office. Sit down, dear. Just take the notes like I told you."

Melody was confused. Didn't he see her nodding her head? She nodded again, more vigorously this time. Still nothing. By now her head was beginning to hurt from shaking it up and down.

The two men were speaking now in low tones. The muffled voices continued on and on. Something was not right, but Melody didn't know what it was. She stood to move closer.

"She can identify you, you fool!" It was Mr. Wilson's voice. "She heard everything you told Lee about killing Prescott. And that bumbling idiot didn't even do that right. Prescott is still alive!"

Melody took a step toward the men, but she was very dizzy.

"You…knew…" She could barely get the words out.

"Take her out the back way. You made this mess, you take care of it."

"You said there were others? What do we do about them?"

"I'll think of something. Hurry before Miss Kris comes in to see what's happening."

Melody sank to the floor.

fourteen

Garrett was having a hard time making his eyes open. He could hear soft noises coming from other places in the house, but he couldn't distinguish what they were. The bed felt larger to him and it occurred to him that he must be somewhere other than the room he was sharing with Josiah and Aaron.

Then he remembered that Eve was married now, and that Mina and Jake had left it up to the three young men to decide who would get her room. Garrett had insisted that Josiah take it. The oldest Rodwell son had been looking forward to a space of his own, but Josiah was reluctant because he thought Garrett should have it, being a guest and all. Aaron said he'd take it if no one else wanted it.

Garrett felt like his chest was twisted up in a sheet. He tried again to get his eyes to open, but he could only get the eyelids to flicker. He tried to remember what he had just been thinking about. The bed. This wasn't the bed he had been sleeping in. He breathed in deeply. Josiah finally took the other room because Garrett felt it only right and wouldn't hear another word about it. Aaron claimed he was happier with Garrett for a roommate anyway, and all were satisfied. So that must mean he was still in the same room he'd been in all along.

But the bed still wasn't right. There was a lot more room in this bed than the one he had. His head was swimming with confusion.

"Garrett? Are you trying to wake up, Garrett? Come on. You can do it!"

Whose voice was that?

"Gar-rett." The voice almost made his name into a song. He knew that voice! He heard it again, humming something as it moved around the room. He made a valiant effort and got one eye open.

He was right. It was Tuva. But where was he? He forced the other eye to open and he looked around. It was Jake and Mina's room, he remembered it from the *grand tour* of the house. He had only been in it that one time. Why was he here now, in their bed?

"Oh, good! Welcome back, sleepyhead!" Tuva stood over him and smiled. With the blonde braid coiled around her head, Garrett could have sworn he was looking up at an angel. "Are you thirsty? The doctor said you'd want water."

"Mmhmm." It was all Garrett could do to get his vocal chords working.

"Here you go. Just small sips now. Let me sprinkle some drops on your tongue and then I'll give you some more."

He wanted to tell her how much he appreciated it, so he tried clearing his throat. "Good." He managed to squeak out the word and was rewarded with a smile from Tuva.

"Wonderful! You'll be up and back to your old self in no time. I'm going to go get you some broth now. Meanwhile, I think there's someone who wants to poke her head in here and say hello. You don't mind, do you?"

Garrett questioned Tuva with his eyes. Did she mean Harmony?

Tuva smiled as if reading his thoughts. "She's been waiting and waiting."

In only a few moments a younger replica of Tuva stood by the bed, only this time the braided hair was over her shoulder. Harmony smiled down at him, and he saw tears glisten the corners of her eyes.

"Hi," she whispered.

"Hi." He managed to get the word out.

"Don't talk now. Mother says you need to keep still, but I'm so happy you're awake. The doctor says you'll be just fine. We're all praying for you."

A tear slid down her cheek and he frowned.

"Don't…"

She wiped it away. "Oh, they're tears of happiness. I can't help it. I cry more when I'm happy than when I'm sad." She laughed softly. "I have to go now. Mother said only a few seconds, but I'll come back. If you want me to."

"Yes." His voice was a little stronger. "Thanks."

The next time Garrett woke, it was Naomi sitting beside the bed. He found he could turn his head to look at her.

"Hi Garrett!" No whispering for Naomi. "Boy, you sleep a lot. I'll get Tuva."

The young girl rushed from the room and Garrett could hear Tuva trying to hush her. Tuva walked silently into the room and smiled at Garrett.

"So, you think you're ready for that broth now?"

"Yes." He cleared his throat. "Yes, ma'am. I could eat a potful."

Tuva laughed. "That's what I was hoping to hear. We'll start with a bowl and go from there. Be right back."

"Uh, Harmony?"

Tuva stopped at the doorway and looked back at him. "She's at school today, but she'll be here tonight."

Garrett lay back and looked at the ceiling. His chest hurt a little when he moved, but other than that he felt good. He tried to remember what happened, but all he could recall was that a man was going to shoot Mina and he jumped...

"Tuva!" he shouted.

He could hear feet running to the room. Tuva, Naomi, Aaron, Keane, and Jasper all crowded about him.

"What is it? Did you fall? Are you hurt?" Tuva was patting the sheets around him looking for an injury.

"What happened to Mina? Where is she? He was going to shoot her!" Garrett was breathing hard and talking fast.

"She's fine, Garrett. Nothing happened to her, thanks to you." Keane put a calming hand on his shoulder.

"Really?" Garrett's voice was filled with suspicion. "Where is she then?"

Keane pulled up a chair as the others went back to the meal they had hurriedly left when he called. Only Jasper stayed leaning against the doorway.

"Trust me when I say that Mina is fine, Garrett. She and Jake and Melody are in Chicago."

Garrett almost sat up. "Chicago! Why?"

"We have a long story to tell you. Sure you're up to it?"

Chicago

Melody's head hurt abominably when she sat up on the cot where she had been lying. She was very frightened as she sat there trying to recall what had happened and trying to figure out where she was. She knew now that Mr. Wilson had been in on the plot along with Bill Gladstone to take Garrett's inheritance and even to have him killed. She tried to remember what happened in the lawyer's office.

He must have put something in that glass of water. No wonder it tasted so bad.

She still felt groggy and nauseous too. She put her hand to her stomach. If she were to be sick, where? She ran her hand along the cot. It was an iron frame with a flat mattress, topped by an itchy wool blanket. No sheets.

Melody shivered. She was cold and as her head began to clear she could hear strange noises all around her. There were voices and sometimes screams. It made the hair on her neck stand up. There was a scurrying sound nearby, and she had to stifle her own scream. It sounded like a mouse.

Could be a rat.

The thought made her pull her feet up around her but then she felt movement on the cot itself and she jumped to her feet, the effort causing the pain in her head to throb. She put her hands on her temples, trying to ease it.

What is this place? "Lord, where am I? Where are Jake and Mina?"

She wouldn't know how to be free of the place until she understood what it was. With one hand holding her head, she held out her other arm and began to walk forward. Soon she felt a wall. It was cold, and as she ran her hand over it, she discovered it was brick. Moving along the wall she came to a corner. She followed the next wall which was also brick until her legs hit something solid. There was a table.

Melody lowered her arm and cautiously felt along the table until she came to a tin basin. A tin pitcher with water stood beside it. She moved on along the wall. The cot was on the other side and the table on this side. What would the fourth side of the room hold?

When she reached the end of the wall and came to the corner, she pulled her hand back and stopped in unbelief. Slowly she reached her hand out again. Iron bars, cold and thick and strong, ran the width of the opening to her cell, her prison.

She was in a jail?

She walked her hands over the bars until she came to the door. She could feel where the hinges were and she tried pulling on the door. As expected, it was locked. The voices were louder now, people were moaning, some wailing, some screaming.

What was the reason for putting her here? She couldn't help but think that the lawyers would want her dead, not in prison where she could talk to someone. Then another more frightening thought occurred to her.

Was this an insane asylum? She had heard of them. Maybe the men had convinced a judge that she needed to be committed. She felt bile rise in her throat and she barely made it to the basin in time.

"Dear Lord, save me!" Jasper, help!

fifteen

Chicago

"I don't like leaving Melody alone like this. She shouldn't have to prove anything to that man. Who does he think he is giving her *tests* to prove she's really blind?"

"Calm down, Mina. I think it's a good idea for Melody to show him that she really can identify Bill Gladstone. You and I can too, but we didn't hear him plan a murder like she did. Try not to worry. He's a lawyer; he knows what to do."

Jake said the words to his wife, but he wasn't sure he believed them himself. He thought it would be an easy matter to get Bill Gladstone arrested and to straighten out the matter of Garrett's inheritance before it was stolen. He had no idea that the papers they produced wouldn't be enough and that the lawyer would insist on testing Melody to see if she really could identify the man.

They were sitting in a back room of the lawyer's building. Mr. Wilson thought it best that Bill Gladstone not stumble upon them in the front offices and try to make a run for it. It made sense, but the longer they sat there, the more uncomfortable Jake became.

"Oh!"

Mina jumped at Jake's exclamation. "What's the matter?"

"I forgot about the cab driver returning for us. It's been about an hour, hasn't it? You stay here. I'm going to check to see if he's waiting."

"But you can't let Bill Gladstone see you."

"I'll be careful. There's a hallway out there that has to lead to a back door somewhere. I'll circle around and check the street out front that way. Be back soon."

Jake found his way out of the building without too much trouble, but discovered that one building butted up against another, so for him to get to the street he had to walk some distance until he came to a corner. His long strides normally got him to places quickly, but here he had to weave his way through the people walking up and down the sidewalks. Finally he got to the street in front of the lawyer's office. He looked for the cab and spotted it not far from the entrance to the building, so he made his way to it. The cab driver seemed surprised that he came from a different direction, but he nodded and tipped his hat to Jake.

"It's going to take a bit longer, I'm afraid. I'll pay you now and could you come back again in say, half an hour?"

"No problem, sir. Thank you, sir. Uh, I know it's none of my business, sir, but did the young lady become ill?"

Jake stared at the man. "What young lady? You mean Melody? The lady with my wife and me? Why do you say that? What do you know?"

"I had a fare on the next street over, sir, and I saw what looked like your friend being carried out the back of the building, sir."

Jake stared at the man. Shock and sudden anger hit him like a physical force.

"Wait right here! Don't move!" Jake shouted as he tore up the steps and crashed through the doorway to the offices of Wilson & Krause. The secretary jumped to her feet, but he charged past her and threw open the door to Mr. Wilson's office, sending it crashing against the wall.

"Where is she?" Jake shouted.

Mr. Wilson was shoving papers into a briefcase but stopped when he saw the look on Jake's face. Jake crossed the room in two strides and grabbed the lawyer by the collar, pulling him across the desk. "Where's Melody? What have you done to her?"

The older man was gasping for air, and the secretary and some men from the other offices rushed in and tried to pull Jake off Mr. Wilson, but he shoved himself free of them. The men staggered back, some falling.

"MINA!" His shout rang through the building. "Get our things; we're going to the police!" He never let go of the lawyer, but pulled him and his briefcase along with him. "Out of my way!" He commanded the others. They stepped back, afraid to tackle the enraged man.

Mina came running, her arms full of coats and her bag and Melody's. "What's happening? What are you doing, Jake?"

"Get in the cab, Mina. We're taking Mr. Wilson for a lesson in the law."

"Where's Melody?"

"That's what he's going to tell us."

Melody tried to squelch the fear that kept trying to take control of her body. She shook with it. She was cold and kept rubbing her hands up and down her arms to warm herself. She stood in the middle of her cell, not willing to risk contact with whatever was scuttling about on the floor and cot.

Think! Someone has to come along sooner or later. All you have to do is explain the situation and everything will be fine.

She was not encouraged by her thoughts. Her blindness had been the cause of many terrifying moments in her life. Facing the unknown was almost a daily thing for her and she had her shares of hazards along the way, but this—being locked in a cell, buried away in a huge city, and not having anyone know where she was—this was the worst she'd experienced. She thought again of being in the root cellar, not knowing if Jasper were alive or not. That had also been terrifying, but she knew her father and brothers would come looking for her then, and somehow, she knew Jake and Mina would look for her now.

If they're alive.

She couldn't stop the thought from forming in her mind. The two crooked lawyers were not going to let them live. Jake and Mina could certainly bear witness against them. Maybe the reason she was still alive was because she couldn't see them. But, no. They still knew she could identify them. Why then was she still alive?

The moaning from the other cells was scaring her more than her own thoughts. *"Lord, why is this happening? What good can possibly come from it?"*

A verse about thankfulness in Thessalonians popped into her head. She didn't want to feel thankful right now. She was in trouble! But the verse came to her mind as verses often did. "In everything give thanks: for this is the will of God in Christ Jesus concerning you." She remembered the sermon Jake gave when he said, "The verse says *in* everything; not *for* everything." He went on to say that we should be thankful for all things, but here, it was to be thankful no matter what your situation.

Melody remembered how he used the example of Paul and Silas. For preaching the Gospel, they were beaten and many stripes were laid upon them, the passage in Acts sixteen read. Then they were thrown into the inner prison and their feet were made fast in the stocks.

Melody bowed her head as she recalled what happened next. The two men, though they were bleeding and beaten, prayed and sang praises to God. The verse said, "…and the prisoners heard them." Later as a result, a prison guard believed on the Lord Jesus Christ and was saved.

Prayer flowed out of her. No longer was she asking God *why?* She just wanted to praise him for saving her. No matter what happened to her on this earth, she had a heavenly home waiting for her with her Redeemer. It was the most natural thing after talking with the Lord for her to raise her head and begin to sing:

> *Amazing grace! How sweet the sound*
> *That saved a wretch like me!*
> *I once was lost, but now am found;*
> *Was blind, but now I see.*

With confidence and clarity her voice rang out through the prison walls, just as Paul and

Silas's must have thousands of years before. The moaning and wailing and the screaming ceased. There was peace and quiet and a hushed reverence as Melody proclaimed God's grace through every word of the song.

She never paused as she moved on from one soothing hymn to another. Her voice echoed through the cold walls and down the corridors. Her love for her Lord reached everyone who heard her.

"Jake! Jake! Listen!"

Jake looked up from leaning over the desk of the police officer in front of him. His face was red with the exertion of trying to tell his story to yet another policeman, each time a higher ranking one than the one before. His impatience at their inactivity to hunt for Melody was increasing and he was about to go out and tear the city apart himself.

"Jake, that's Melody singing!" Mina was yelling now and Jake lifted his head to listen. The policemen gathered in the office also turned to the sound. One of them reached for a key and opened the door that led to the cells. Melody's voice floated to them from far down the row of bars.

"It's her! That's the girl, officer. The girl they kidnapped!" Jake tried to push past the men in the room, but they stopped him, having to forcibly hold him back. "I tell you it's her!"

The officer at the desk looked through the papers again. "If what you're saying is true, that she was kidnapped, then how did she end up here?"

Jake was at the end of his patience. "I don't know how or why she's in there, but she is and she shouldn't be."

The officer indicated that the door be shut.

"No!" Mina screamed. "Melody! Melody! We're here!"

"You," he pointed at Mina. "Sit down and be quiet. We're going to get to the bottom of this." He turned to the men. "Do you know who is singing back there?"

"No sir."

"Find out. Get her name and get the man who brought her in."

"Yes sir."

Jake dropped to the bench beside Mina. They were both weary from the fight of trying to get someone to listen to them. He begged the police officer to get a judge to look over the papers, and he told them that Bill Gladstone needed to be arrested for attempted murder and that the papers were their proof. The story had been told and retold. He was glad, at least, that they were holding Mr. Wilson until they knew more.

Mina was quiet beside him. "Did you hear what she was singing, Jake?" she asked gently.

He shook his head, too tired to answer.

"She was singing that new song that she and Tuva and Harmony did together not long ago at church. You remember it, Jake. Listen, the words that touched you the most were, 'But the Master of the sea heard my despairing cry, from the waters lifted me, now safe am I.' Melody is safe, Jake. No matter where she is, she's safe in Christ. We have to let the Lord fight this battle for us."

Jake leaned forward and rubbed at his head. "You're a good wife, Mina. I needed to hear that. What was the name of that hymn? 'Love Lifted Me'? Melody is letting Christ's love for her lift her from the despair around her. She's quite a woman."

A policeman hurried in and reported to the officer behind the desk. Instead of jumping up to demand what was going on, Jake sat where he was and waited. The officer glanced at him a few times while he listened to the man, then finally motioned for him and for Mina to come forward.

"This man said he found the lady, drunk and disorderly, by the railroad tracks. She was stumbling about like she couldn't see where she was going."

Very quietly and slowly Jake spoke. "She's *blind*. And she's never been drunk in her life. Did the man smell anything on her?"

The officer looked at the man and received a negative shake of his head. Then the young man spoke. "Sir, I have a boy outside who may know something about her."

"A boy?"

"A beggar, sir. He says he found her in danger of being hit by a train."

Mina gasped and Jake's fists clenched.

"Shall I bring him in, sir?"

"Yes."

They waited while the policeman stepped outside and watched him lead a young boy into the room. "He's a blind boy, sir." The man explained.

"Why, he's the boy from the train station!" Mina knelt down to him and took his shoulders to turn his face toward her. "He asked for some money, but I didn't realize he was blind." She brushed the hair from the boy's face.

"Do you know what happened to the lady at the train yard?" The officer spoke to him.

"I don't want to get in trouble."

"You won't, but you know you shouldn't be begging from the good people who go in and out of there."

Mina frowned at the officer.

"Just tell us what happened to the lady."

"I heard a cabbie coming so I hid by the station. Thought maybe I could get a coin or two from someone getting on the trains."

He ducked his head, waiting for another reprimand.

"Go on."

"I heard a man grunting like he was carrying something heavy. He walked to the back of the station and put something down. I stayed hid 'til he was gone then I scooted over there to see what he put there. It was a person! He put a person right down on the tracks, mister! Honest! I knew a train was going to come soon. I know all the trains," he added proudly. "So I tried to get the person to get up off the track and I found out it was a woman and she wouldn't wake up. I tried and tried, and finally I started pulling her off the track 'cuz I could hear the train was coming! I think I bumped her head because she groaned something fierce then she sat up all on her own. I said to her that she had to get up and move and she got up. She couldn't seem to walk too good and that's when the policeman came and took her away." He stopped like he was out of breath.

Jake watched the officer's face as he studied the boy. Surely he'd release Melody now!

"How did you know it was a policeman who took her away?"

The boy ducked his head again. "I know when the police are around 'cuz they always take that stick they carry and run it across the fence there at the depot. I know that sound real good."

"You know it because you run and hide when you hear it?"

The boy nodded.

"Did the man who dropped the lady off say anything? Did you hear his voice?"

The boy thought a minute. "Yes, sir, he did. He said 'Blind girl struck by train. That will make a good headline.' And then he said some words I can't say with this lady here."

The officer straightened. "Go get the woman." He ordered.

Jake breathed an audible sigh of relief then reached for Mina and hugged her.

The officer spoke again. "Boy, would you stay here a little longer? I want you to tell me if you recognize the voice of the man when we bring him in the room."

Jake turned to the officer, Mina still held close in his arms. "You've got Bill Gladstone?"

The officer nodded. "We haven't been idle, Mr. Rodwell." He looked at the boy again. "How about it? Will you help us?"

The boy scowled. "What's *recknize* mean?"

For the first time Jake saw the officer smile. "It means, you tell me if it's the same man when you hear him speak, okay?"

"Okay."

The door to the cells opened, and Jake and Mina and the officers could hear people calling out to the woman being led down the corridor.

"Bless you, Miss!"
"Thank you! Thank you!"
"Voice of an angel!"
"God love you, Miss!"
"You've given us hope! Thank you!"

Moments later Melody was led into the room and the door was closed behind her. Instead of panic, that Jake feared he would see on her face, there was only bewilderment at the circumstances. One hand was on the policeman's arm and her other was held over her heart as if she were protecting herself from whatever was to come next. Her hair had come loose from its braid, and her dress was dirty and the skirt torn.

"Melody!"

Mina rushed to her, and Melody grasped onto her as if she'd never let go. That's when the tears started to flow.

"Mina, is Jake all right?"

"I'm here, Mel. We're both okay, but how are you? Are you hurt? We're so sorry we let you go into that office alone."

"I'm not hurt, just bruised and have an awful headache. It's not your fault that Mr. Wilson was also a crook. He drugged me by putting something into the water he gave me then he told that Bill Gladstone to get rid of me. I don't know what happened after that until I woke up here. Thank the Lord you two are safe. I prayed and prayed."

"Uh, Miss?"

Melody turned to the man who spoke, but Jake saw that she did not release her hold on Mina. "Yes?"

"If I could get a statement from you about what happened?"

"Officer," Jake's voice was firm as he intervened. "I think you just did. If there's nothing else, I need to get these ladies to a hotel. They've been through quite an ordeal in your city."

The officer held up a hand despite the glare Jake gave him. "There is one more thing. Please, no one say anything. Just stay where you are for one more minute." He motioned to a man. The man nodded and opened a door and in walked Bill Gladstone, his hands in cuffs.

The young lawyer was red in the face. He surveyed the room with a quick, sweeping glance then demanded. "What's the meaning of this, officer? I'll have your badge! Who are these people? I've never seen them before. What's this all about?"

Melody stiffened and dug her hands into Mina's arms.

"Well?" The officer asked.

In unison Melody and the beggar boy answered. "It's him!"

"Take him away."

They could hear Bill Gladstone yelling as the men led him out of the room. For a moment it was still, then Mina said in a pained voice, "You can let go now, Melody."

"Oh, I'm sorry, Mina!" Melody released the grip she had on Mina.

Jake stepped forward and took Melody's arm. "Let's get you out of here."

"Wait!" Melody stopped them. "Who was that who spoke? Is there a child here?"

"Yes, it's the boy from the train station, the one who asked for some change. Do you remember him?" Mina explained.

Melody rubbed at her forehead as she thought. "He helped me. I remember now. He pulled me off the tracks. I could hear a train was coming, in fact, I could *feel* it coming. Where is he?" She knelt down and reached out her arms. Mina put her hand on the boy's shoulder and led him to Melody.

"He's blind too, Melody."

Melody felt the boy's shoulders and ran a hand lightly over his head and face. "You're blind? Me too!" She took his hand and brought it to her face and let him touch her. "That was a very brave thing you did today. You saved my life. Thank you." She pulled him into her arms and hugged him.

The boy sniffed. "You don't smell too good."

Melody laughed. "I've been in a very smelly place. And just so you know, you don't smell so good either. You have a name?"

"Not really. People just mostly call me Boy, but I have a real name. It's Edward, but I don't like that. I like Eddie better."

"Eddie, huh? Well, Eddie, since we both don't smell very good, how about we take you back to the hotel with us and get you a good meal and a bath? Would you like that?"

"Really? And sleep in a bed too?"

"Yes, and sleep in a bed too." Melody stood up with her hand on Eddie's shoulder. "Okay with you, Jake?"

"Absolutely."

The officer cleared his throat. "The boy should really be brought to an—"

"Not tonight." Jake's statement was met with silence until finally the officer nodded.

"Come on, Eddie. Officer, we'll stop by in the morning, so if there's anything else you need, we'll take care of it then. And thank you. And I apologize for my impatience."

"Understandable, sir. See you tomorrow."

sixteen

Ulen

Garrett walked with Harmony down the long driveway of the Rodwell farm. It felt good to be up and about again, even though he was quite weak. It was already October and Harmony was free from school for two weeks as the children were needed at home to pick the potato crops.

"I'm worried about them, Harmony. Jake and Mina and Melody have been gone too long. Something's happened."

"Mom and Dad are worried too. None of us have much experience with large cities. Well, Jake and my dad have a little, but that was a long time ago. Anything could happen and we would have no way of knowing. I keep hoping they'll send another telegram, or that they'll call the telephone in town and someone will come out here with a message for us, but nothing. The one telegram we got a couple days after they got to Chicago just said they had more business to take care of." Harmony's voice shook. "At least we know they got there."

Garrett slid his good arm around her shoulder and she leaned into him. "Even though your dad is worried, he talks to me about trusting the Lord through this. It's hard for me to understand how to trust the Lord. It's so new to me."

Harmony looked up at him. "I'm so glad you put your faith in Jesus, Garrett." She wiped at her eyes where tears had formed. "Dad's right, of course. The Lord knows where they are, and we can trust that whatever the outcome of all this is, he will see us through it."

"But we can still worry?"

"I think being concerned about someone you love is how you show you care for them."

Garrett pulled Harmony into an embrace. "I know I care about you, and I am awfully glad you've been concerned about me."

They stood together for a moment then Harmony moved away but took Garrett's hand as they continued their walk. "I do care for you, Garrett, and that's something I wanted to talk to you about." She hesitated.

"Yes?"

"I just want you to know that you don't have to feel…you don't have to stay here…I mean, with your inheritance and all, things will change for you, and you don't have to…"

Garrett stopped again but Harmony didn't look up at him. "First of all, I don't even know if there will be an inheritance, and second, well, I'll admit that I started thinking of all the grand gestures I could make if I had a lot of money and how I could impress you with it, but when I was in that bed and my life was possibly over, I knew all I wanted was to know where I would spend my eternity. I was scared of hell.

"So many times I had heard the salvation message through all of you, but I resisted it because I thought I was a much better man than my father, and maybe in my mind I was trying to prove it by not believing the same message he did. I don't know. But in those last moments while Jake explained it all to me again, I knew I needed Christ's gift to me as much as anyone else does."

Garrett breathed deeply. "And it has changed my perspective on so many things. I resisted using the name Prescott at first, knowing what my father had been like, but then I understood that he became a new man, if only for a few moments before he died. Now the name has a different meaning to me as I see Grandpa and Grandma Prescott and Mina. I'm proud to have their name. And this inheritance—my mother fled from her father's money because my father desired it more than her. I don't want money to be my reason to exist, I want to know more about God and about life and I want to learn it here, with you."

The last words were spoken with emphasis, and Harmony looked up and saw the truth in Garrett's eyes. She closed her eyes as he bent his head toward her and sealed his words with a kiss, a promise of a future together.

"Excuse me."

They both jumped at the words and pulled apart when Jasper walked his horse up to them. He was grinning and pushed the brim of his hat back on his head. "Looks like you're feeling better." He commented to Garrett.

Garrett just grinned back at him.

"You going somewhere, Jasper?" Harmony pointed to the bag on the back of the saddle.

Jasper nodded. "I can't wait another day with no word from them." His tone was now serious. "I'm going there, to Chicago, and I'm not coming back without them."

But Garrett was shaking his head. "You can't. I mean, I know Chicago and you can't just find someone. You have to know where to look. Listen, I have a better idea. Call that number for the lawyer's office again."

"We've tried that, but they're not talking, you know that. All they do is say they can't give out information over the phone.

Listen, I'll send telegrams every other day while I'm there. That way you'll know I'm okay and I can update you on my progress." Jasper pulled his hat forward again, but Garrett could see the misery in the man's eyes. "I have to find Melody. I have to."

"Wait, Jasper. There's someone coming. Over there." Harmony pointed across the fields.

They turned to see a man on horseback coming down the road.

"It looks like Grandpa Thomsen. Maybe he has some news."

Jasper swung down from the saddle and waited with the others while the older man came toward them. Once the man saw them, he began waving a paper in his hand.

"Got a telegram!" he called.

Jasper dropped the horse's reins and ran to him. He reached for the paper and read it quickly then shouted to Harmony and Garrett, "They're on their way! They should be here tomorrow!"

The joyful group made their way to the Wheatly farm where Keane and Tuva and the others gathered to hear the good news.

"I wish it said more about why it has taken so long, but we'll just have to wait and hear the story from them when they get here." Keane said. He slapped Grandpa Thomsen on the back. "Thank you for riding over to bring that to us. You are the bearer of good tidings!"

Grandpa stirred the coffee cup before him. "We've all been praying. I think Ole Aselson is the happiest of all of us to hear the news because I've been going in every day, hovering around the telegraph office and sitting outside his store just waiting to hear something. He said I was starting to drive the customers away."

The others laughed, knowing their grandpa was joking, but understanding the concern he also had for his loved ones.

"Well, now that we know for sure they'll be home, we have a lot to do." Tuva took off her apron and reached for a coat.

"Where are you going?" Keane stood up, puzzled at his wife's behavior.

"I'm going to give Mina's house a top to bottom cleaning. Come on, Harmony." And she headed out the door.

Harmony and Garrett followed her out, and Keane sat down and shook his head. "Women!" he said, causing Grandpa Thomsen to laugh. Then Jasper got up and excused himself.

"I got some cleaning to do myself," he explained over his shoulder.

Keane thought for a moment. "Guess I better get Jake's barn tidied up too. Come on, boys."

Grandpa Thomsen sat at the table alone and sipped his coffee and helped himself to another of Tuva's delicious doughnuts.

They were all at the train station the next day, scrubbed clean and wearing their finest clothes. Jasper had a small bouquet of flowers in his hand. He had stopped along the way to pick the final blooms of the season.

It seemed the whole town had come out to witness the return of the Rodwells and Melody. All had heard of the attempt on Garrett's life as well as of the abduction of Jasper and Melody. The women in town had taken turns bringing meals to the Rodwell farm while Garrett recovered from his surgery, a witness of the bond the small community had for its own.

Jasper couldn't stand still in one place. He paced up and down the platform until Keane pointed to the flowers he was carrying. They were almost mangled by his swinging them back and forth with each stride. He sheepishly set them down on a bench beside Garrett and Harmony and took off walking again. Where was that train?

It had been almost two weeks since Melody left with Jake and Mina. Jasper had been against her going from the start, not wanting her to have to face the unknowns in a big city with her blindness. It had been hard for him to wonder and worry every day what might be happening to her, and now as he waited for her return, he knew more than ever that he wanted her by his side for the rest of his life. Being apart from her was sheer torture.

When the train whistle announced its approach, Jasper was down the street. He ran to the station and side-stepped his way through the crowd gathered to get to the Wheatlys. At the last moment he remembered the flowers and turned to find Harmony holding them with a smile on her face. She handed them over and gave him one of her cheeky winks.

Jasper grinned. It was just what he needed to relax. He shook his shoulders and swung his neck to relieve the tightness then he watched the train as it slowly made its stop. He searched every window for a glimpse of Melody and finally saw her. His breath came out in a whoosh of relief.

She's home. She's safe. "Thank you, Lord!"

The station man motioned for the crowd to move back to allow the passengers to exit, but it was futile once Mina and Jake stepped down. The crowd surged forward. Naomi rushed to her mother with a loud squeal of delight, and Josiah and Aaron were close on her heels, followed by Eve and Torkel. The family reunion brought tears to the eyes of some, but Jasper kept his eyes on the platform behind them.

Where is she?

Jake turned then and reached for a gloved hand that appeared. Jasper held his breath. Yes, that was her! Melody took the hand and descended the steps, but before Jasper could get to her, she turned and took the hand of a young boy. An older gentleman spoke to her and she answered him as he stepped down from the train behind her. Jasper watched as Keane and Tuva embraced their daughter. She was hugged and was hugging them back, but Jasper saw her turn her head as if listening for something. He reached her side.

"There you are," she said.

He scooped her into his arms and swung her around. How she knew he was beside her, he'd never know, and right at this moment he didn't care. She was home.

"Ole Jasperson! You put me down! There are people here!" Melody tried to sound stern, but she was smiling and laughing at the same time. Everyone watching joined in and the greetings continued, but Jasper kept Melody's hand in his and wouldn't let go.

Jake raised his hand for attention and eventually the crowd quieted. "Thank you for the warm welcome. We're very happy to be back, and I think I speak for all three of us when I say that we never plan to leave Ulen, Minnesota, again!"

People laughed and clapped at this statement. The crowd began to disperse until only the Wheatly and Rodwell families remained. Jake spoke again. "Mr. Krause came back with us to discuss business with

Garrett and to finalize the issue of his inheritance."

The older man had waited quietly in the background through the noisy welcome, and he now stepped forward and tipped his hat.

Jake continued. "We thought it might be best if we gathered at the hotel lobby to talk. Mr. Krause would like to get the business done tonight and be on the train back to Chicago tomorrow."

"Fine," Keane put in. "We already have the dining room reserved there as we thought it would be a good time to have our dinner and talk before we all headed for home. I'm sure you have a lot to tell us, and we figured you would rather say it to the whole group rather than have to repeat it over and over."

"Good thinking." Jake looked around him at his friends and family. "It's good to be home."

The group headed in the direction of the Orient Hotel, but Melody held back beside Jasper. He squeezed her hand and she leaned into him. He smiled. Everything was right again.

"Jasper, there's something I need to ask you before we go to the hotel."

Jasper didn't allow her to continue as he pulled her into his arms and kissed her. She pulled away.

"Jasper! Not here!"

"There's no one around, honey. I missed you so much!"

Her voice softened. "I missed you too. There were times when I thought I'd never, pardon the expression, *see* you again."

He laughed with her.

"Jake will explain what we've been through, so I won't try to tell you it all now, but there is one very important matter I have to discuss with you."

"Anything." Jasper saw her seriousness and watched her face closely.

"The boy. Did you see the boy with us?"

"Yes. Why?"

"Jasper, he's an orphan, he's blind, and he saved my life."

"What? Your life?"

Melody quickly continued. "That's the quick story, and I promise to tell you the details later, but what I need to ask you is…"

"You want him."

Melody blinked at a tear. "You always seem to guess what I'm going to say. Yes, I want him, but only if it's something you are willing to consider. It's a huge decision to ask you to not only take on a blind wife, but also a blind son."

She didn't go on and Jasper knew there were many details she could share and ways she could try to convince him, but he didn't need to know them to make his decision. If

Melody felt it was the right thing to do, he was happy to do it.

He pulled her close again and she didn't resist. "You're going to make a great mother," he whispered to her. "I will do my best to be a good father. Let's go meet my son."

"Oh, Jasper!" She wiped at her eyes. "You do beat all. And to think I thought you were interested in Miss Emerson."

"Miss Emerson has a wart on her nose."

It took time for Jake, Mina, and Melody to tell about their trip. Many times they had to stop and go over something again as questions were asked and exclamations were made. Disbelief and shock were on the faces of the listeners.

Garrett was the most affected. This was all because of him. He never imagined that his coming to this little town would cause so much trouble for the people he had come to know and love. He looked around as he saw Jasper's pained expression when learning of what Melody had gone through. He saw Keane comfort Tuva as tears flowed down her face. He looked at Harmony and saw the shock and confusion of a girl who had never known such cruelty and hate. And he had brought it all here and made them all experience it firsthand.

Jake asked Mr. Krause to finish the story for him and he sat down beside Mina. Naomi scooted her chair closer to her father and put her arms around him and hugged him tightly. Garrett looked on in sympathy for the young girl's need for reassurance that her father was all right.

"I can only give my most profound apologies for the despicable behavior of members of my law office. Be assured that both men have been prosecuted, tried, and found guilty of their crimes and are now incarcerated. The reason for the lengthy stay of your family in Chicago was so that we could get their testimonies in court before they returned.

"We also have in custody in the city the man named Lee who was captured here in Minnesota, and the young woman who was prepared to masquerade as a relative of Mr. Prescott. They, too, will pay for their crimes. Now, as to the matter of Mr. Prescott's inheritance." He turned to Garrett. "Shall we find a private place to conduct our business?"

Garrett hesitated then raised a hand to halt the lawyer. He stood. His face was somber as he faced the people he had come to love and respect. They were all there including Grandpa and Grandma Prescott and Tuva's parents, Grandpa and Grandma Thomsen. They were family.

"Before we get into that, I just want to say..." He had to pause to compose himself. "I need to say that I am deeply sorry for what you have all had to go through because of me."

Immediately protests began, but Garrett put up a hand to stop them.

"No, let me finish. I came here to find answers, to find out who I was, and to learn something about the man who left my mother. I found you. You took me at my word, you welcomed me into your homes, and you made me a member of your families and your community despite the fact that I was the son of a man who committed evil against you. I have never had anything like this before in my life. I thank you for accepting me.

"Then you showed me why you care the way you do. You showed me that it was because of God, of Jesus Christ, that you can love someone, the son of someone who almost destroyed you." Garrett looked at Jake and Keane.

"I didn't want to hear about God. I didn't want to accept what my father accepted because I didn't want to do anything like he did. But I'm so glad you didn't give up on me. As Melody told me, 'I was blind, but now I see'.

"But all this trouble that has come to you since has been because of me." Again protests were raised, but Garrett hushed them. "I don't deserve an inheritance. I don't even want it. It seems to represent the source of the problems in my life, and I don't want it to cause more problems. I don't know what to do. Again, I'm sorry."

He sat down but couldn't look at the people around him.

Keane reached for Garrett's uninjured arm and squeezed it. "None of us deserve anything, Garrett. But whether this inheritance is a nickel or a million dollars, it's yours. Be thankful for it and use it wisely to the glory of God. Money isn't a sin. The Bible tells us that the love of money is the root of all evil. Keep your eyes on the Lord and it won't become a problem.

"As to you apologizing for what's happened these last few weeks, I think I can speak for all of us when I say we'd gladly face it all again if it meant we could see you come to Christ. Nothing else on this earth matters but that."

"We love you, Garrett." Mina came to him and put her arm around him. "I am so happy you came here. I have no regrets."

Others added their agreement. Garrett was astounded by their attitudes and had to brush away tears with the back of his hand. He laughed, surprising them. "As long as I have you all in such a generous, forgiving mood..."

They laughed with him as he turned first to Keane. "May I have your permission to ask your daughter to marry me?"

The room hushed as Keane nodded his approval. Garrett turned to Harmony, who stared at him, her eyes huge.

"I have no idea if I'm a rich man or a poor man, but before any of us know, would you do me the honor of being my wife, just as I am?"

Harmony, the coquettish and flirtatious girl, could only nod shyly.

"What did she say?" Melody's impatience to know couldn't be contained.

Everyone laughed as Harmony jumped to her feet and into Garrett's arms, receiving an "Ouch!" in response.

"I said yes. Yes!"

It was after the lawyer finished discussing his business with Garrett that he came to where Melody, Jasper, and Eddie were sitting. Jasper and Eddie had been getting acquainted over their evening meal.

"Excuse me, I hate to interrupt, but Miss Wheatly has asked that I prepare adoption papers, and we should get these matters settled before I have to leave tomorrow."

"Please, sit down." Jasper pulled out a chair.

Mr. Krause pulled some papers from his satchel. "In these matters, it has to be confirmed that the child has no other relatives who could take him in. We checked at the orphanage where Edward had lived and learned that he was brought there as an infant after his parents died of diphtheria. He left the orphanage on his own—I guess you could say he escaped—"

"I didn't like them people. They locked me in a room, and they hurt me sometimes."

Melody reached for Eddie and put her arm around him, but she said nothing as the lawyer continued.

"Yes, well, from what the police told me, the boy has pretty much lived on the streets and fended for himself ever since."

"How old are you, Eddie?" Jasper asked.

"I don't know."

The lawyer looked through his papers. "It would seem he's seven years old, according to these documents."

There was compassion mixed with admiration in Jasper's voice when he spoke quietly. "And blind too."

Mr. Krause nodded in understanding. "Since there are no other relatives, Edward can be adopted, but he must go to a married couple, not a single woman, you see. Miss Wheatly has told me that you two intend to get married." He waited for Jasper's confirmation.

"That's right."

"Are you in agreement to adopt the boy?"

"Yes, sir." There was no hesitation. Melody slipped her hand in Jasper's.

"It is not the usual case to allow the adoption to go through before the marriage, but under the circumstances, I will have you sign the documents now. The only condition is that you must marry within one month. Is that agreeable?"

"Very agreeable. We can be married right now, for that matter."

"Jasper."

"Okay, we'll take a few days to get ready, but we will definitely be married within a month."

It was a joyous trip to their homes. Night was settling in and Melody breathed deeply of the night air. It was cold and crisp, but welcoming. She wondered if she could ever forget the stench of the jail. Her experience had given her a deeper appreciation for her home and her family. She snuggled closer to Jasper's side. How she loved him! She had little doubt that he would accept Eddie as his own. How many men could be counted on for that!

She smiled as she listened to Eddie talking to her parents, most likely telling them again how he had rescued her from the train. He was tucked in between them on the wagon seat. Their reaction to having a readymade grandson had been priceless and endearing. Eddie's reaction when Keane told him that he'd teach him to ride a horse had brought tears to her eyes when he reached for Keane and threw his arms around him. At the moment she could tell that he was peppering them with questions about everything related to horses.

Jasper had asked so many questions about her experience that Melody was worn out reliving it all, but she knew he had the right to know and that they could then put it behind them. He had one more question.

"Why didn't you send more telegrams? We were all desperate to know what was happening."

Melody yawned. "The truth is that we were out of money. Everything was so expensive, Jasper. Once Mr. Krause learned that we would have to move out of the hotel until all the hearings were over because of lack of funds, he took over everything for us including our meals, but Jake didn't feel we should ask for money to send telegrams. It just didn't seem right."

Jasper nodded in understanding. "I'm so glad you're home. Happy?" He asked in her ear.

She nodded against him. "And tired. I think I'll need a week to catch up on sleep."

"Not allowed. You have a wedding to plan."

Melody nudged him with her elbow then she pulled back. "Jasper, what would you think if we made it a double wedding with Garrett and Harmony?"

"Sure. If you're okay with that, I am. Have you talked with Harmony yet?"

"No, not yet. I'm so happy for her, Jasper. Do you think they might live in Chicago?" She couldn't control a shudder that went through her. Jasper pulled her close again.

"I'm sure that not all of that city is as horrible as what you experienced."

"No, I know that. I was thinking of how much I'd miss her if she lived far away."

"I know, but it will be up to them to decide." He changed the subject. "I like Eddie. He's a little rough around the edges, but he's a good kid."

"I thought you were going to choke on your steak when he asked if he could call you Dad."

Jasper laughed. "It took me by surprise, alright. He's already calling you Mom. I love you so much, Melody."

"I love you too. Thank you, Jasper."

seventeen

One issue Garrett wanted to make clear to the lawyer was that no matter what it cost, all the expenses of the trip made by Jake and the ladies would come out of his inheritance. Mr. Krause calmly explained that his firm had already taken care of it and that none of it would be taken from Gordon Fairfax's estate.

"I felt it was our obligation and duty to do so since it was our firm's actions that caused the trouble," the lawyer had explained. He ventured further to assure him that any medical expenses would also be covered.

Garrett recalled the conversation as he walked the horse into town. He had been stunned by the revelation of the amount he would be receiving and the knowledge that there was a house and lands as well. At some point he would have to make a trip there to decide what to do about it. For now, Mr. Krause would handle the care of the home.

When he asked Garrett if he should keep the servants on for the time being, Garrett had confessed that he knew nothing of such matters. It was all so overwhelming.

Today he had to go to the bank and sign papers to transfer some money. He and Harmony had many decisions to make. He had to smile to himself. She was as out of her element about all this as he was.

Town was quiet, possibly because it was such a cold, windy day. A few people were on the boardwalk, moving from one store to the next. Garrett spotted a surrey loaded down with furniture and goods. It had side curtains, and as they flapped in the wind, he could see a row of children lined up on the back seat. On the front seat was a woman holding a well-bundled baby in her arms, and a young girl about ten years old held the lines directing the movements of two slow, plodding horses. He smiled at the girl and she shyly smiled back. Just then her mother spoke to her.

"Olive! The lines!"

Garrett jumped down from the horse and ran to the surrey. The moment's distraction had caused the girl named Olive to slacken her grip on the reins and the long lines had become wrapped around the axle of the buggy wheel. Even now the horses were beginning a tight circle.

"Whoa there!" Garrett caught the horses' bridles and stopped them. He gathered the lines and untwisted them then handed them back to the girl who looked at him wide-eyed. The mother thanked him and they moved off north of town. He heard the girl call out to the horses, "Git, Cub! C'mon, Polly!"

"That's the Purriers," Ole Asleson explained, coming up behind Garrett. "They're buying a farm in Walworth Township. Nice of you to give the girl a hand."

"She was doing fine, but she looked cold. That wind is really something today." Garrett blew on his hands to thaw them.

"Weather's a funny thing. I've seen years where there's no snow in January and then it's 90° in October. I've seen twenty to thirty foot drifts of snow, 50° below zero, and I've seen morning glories bloom in December. Guess we see our share of wild weather, from dust storms to tornadoes to blizzards, not to mention hail and grasshoppers destroying the crops from time to time. You got to be hardy or stupid to live here." Ole chuckled and walked on.

Garrett thought about what the man said as he made his way to the bank. He didn't know if he was hardy enough, but he didn't agree that people were stupid to make this northern place their home. There were good people here and good land, and he was happy to be here.

His business done at the bank, Garrett headed to the Wheatlys. Harmony had put in her notice at the school and had already been replaced so that she could be free to prepare for their wedding. She and Melody agreed that they wanted to share the day, and Garrett couldn't be happier.

The Wheatly household was in a flurry of activity when Garrett arrived. Fabric was strewn across the dining table, and Tuva and Mina were busily pinning pieces together. Eve was at the sewing machine, pumping her feet as the needle stitched its way through what seemed like miles of satin while Naomi fed the cloth to her in a steady stream. Harmony looked up and smiled at him, but there were pins in her mouth, so she couldn't speak. Melody stepped from the kitchen to offer coffee.

"Save yourself, man!" Keane warned as he and Jasper came in from the back door.

Garrett only grinned.

Soon the table was cleared and the men sat down to warm themselves with the coffee and baked sweets Melody put before them. Eddie, who was constantly at Jasper's side, asked if he could have coffee too.

"Okay, you can today since it's so cold, but you'll use cream in it, young man."

"Oh, boy! And can I have some of that lefse too?"

"Of course."

Garrett watched the boy gobble down the delicacies. His happiness was contagious and a blessing to the others especially when his story had been shared. It got Garrett to thinking about the young girl in town driving the team of horses. Children had a hard life, but that young girl had a family, a buggy full of brothers and sisters to grow up with. Eddie had been fending for himself in a big city with no one to rely on. Thankfully he now would have Jasper and Melody and all the Rodwell and Wheatly clans to share his life. Garrett thought of his own life. At least he had his mother, though their situation was desperate at times.

But Garrett couldn't help thinking of the children on the streets in Chicago. He had been there and seen them. He had walked by the orphanages and had seen the factories. Jake and Mina talked about what they had seen—the children begging for a coin, the ragged, dirty children watching them with hungry eyes.

"If only we could help," Mina had said.

Garrett looked at Harmony laughing at something that Keane said. *She will make a great mother.* He wondered what she would think of the idea forming in his head.

It was really too cold for a walk outside, but Garrett needed to talk to Harmony alone and the small house offered no privacy. But Harmony was game. She bundled up and took his arm and they stepped out into the wind. Behind them he heard Keane say something about 'young love'.

"The barn would offer some protection from the wind," Harmony yelled to him. They couldn't even carry on a conversation as they were nearly blown down the path to the barn. Once inside they looked at each other and laughed. It truly was not a good night for a walk.

"I needed to talk to you about something that's been on my mind." Garrett started right in. He didn't want to keep her out in the cold too long.

"Yes?" Harmony pulled her scarf off her head to listen.

"I've been thinking about children." At Harmony's surprised look and raised color, he laughed. "I mean, I've been thinking about the children in Chicago that Melody and the others have been talking about, the ones with no families."

"The orphans and the street children?"

"Yes. I know we haven't seen my grandfather's house yet, but Mr. Krause says it's quite large with many rooms. I was just thinking…"

"…to make it a home for children?" Harmony finished for him.

"Yes." He watched for her reaction as she considered the idea. "I know we would have to go there and decide for sure after we see the place, and that there would be a lot of legal papers and stuff, but…I don't know…I just can't stop thinking about it."

Harmony smiled and put her hand against his cheek. "You're a good man, Garrett Foxe Prescott. I very much like the idea. If we can help even a few of those children, it would change their lives and ours."

He drew her to him. "And we need to tell them about the love of God and how they can have a life in Christ like we have."

"Yes." His head was lowering now.

"And we'll teach them to sing because music is important."

"It is." Harmony's eyes closed as Garrett got nearer.

"And we'll do the same with our children."

Her eyes flew open. Then he kissed her.

The weather changed as the weather does, so that on the day of the double wedding, the sun was shining and the wind was still. It was decided to move the ceremony outdoors instead of in the small church which would have been standing room only for the number of people expected. Jake and Keane and their sons arrived early and began the task of setting up chairs for their guests and tables for the food that was coming.

Keane paused in his efforts to inspect the results of their labors and found Jake eyeing him, a smirk on his face.

"What are you thinking about?" Keane's eyebrows drew together.

Jake's smile grew. "Can you imagine, when we were back on that ship and Thorpe was lording over us, that one day I would be married to his sister, and you—" He poked Keane on the chest. "—you would have his son for a son-in-law?"

Keane shook his head, reflective in his thoughts. "I am still awed at God's grace and how he can change a person's heart."

Jake peered closer at his friend. "You're not talking about Thorpe or Garrett, are you?"

Keane grinned. "Nope. I'm talking about me."

Melody and Harmony shared their room together for the last time as they prepared for their big day. Their dresses were slightly different from each other, a little more lace on Harmony's, high necks and long sleeves because of the season on both, and Melody's had a row of pearl buttons all down the back. Their veils were the same.

The girls had their tearful moments the night before as they talked together into the night. Harmony and Garrett planned to leave for Chicago after spending a night in the hotel in town. They would investigate Garrett's grandfather's estate and decide if it would be suitable for the children's home they hoped to create. Depending on what steps had to be taken, they may be there for months. The plan after that was to return to Ulen and live in town in a house that they had already purchased.

Melody and Jasper would go straight to his home after the ceremony. They would have a few days alone for a honeymoon then Eddie would join them and they would begin their life as a family.

"Can you believe this is actually going to happen?" Harmony asked.

"Are you nervous?"

"Terrified. Aren't you?"

Melody smiled as she slipped her arm through her sister's. "Absolutely! And I'm happy and sad at the same time."

"I'll miss you, Mel."

Melody sniffed. "Stop it or you'll have me bawling. Let's go get married."

Their father walked them down the grassy aisle, a bride on each arm. Keane first kissed Melody's cheek and gave her hand to Jasper, then he kissed Harmony and handed her over to Garrett. Then he took his place beside Tuva while the couples faced Jake, who was officiating. They had no other attendants as they were witnesses for each other.

Jake beamed with pleasure as he faced not only the four people in front of him, but all their friends and family besides. His short message was clear and quite special.

"I have been asked today to share with you the testimony of each of the young people standing before me. It is their desire more than any other for you—their friends, their families—to know beyond a shadow of a doubt where you will spend eternity. Their happiness in being joined as man and wife is secondary to that request."

Jasper's story of salvation brought laughter from the crowd as Jake related how as a young boy Jasper wanted to know what it was like to be blind like Melody. "After days of wearing a handkerchief around his eyes, his parents had about enough and demanded he take it off. He had been bumping into things, knocking things over, and causing chaos wherever he went. One day he nearly fell out of the hayloft. He was dangling by his fingertips when his father rescued him. The thought of dying scared him and he asked his father how he could be sure he'd go to heaven if he died. His father shared with him that Jesus had died for his sins and rose again and that Jasper needed to believe that message to be saved. Jasper understood that he was a sinner, and that is one thing that I personally can attest to, that Jasper was a sinner."

The crowd laughed again.

"He knew he needed to be saved and he believed right there in the hayloft of his father's barn."

Next Jake told about Melody and Harmony. "I've had the privilege of being the girls' pastor for their entire lives. They told me that in one of my sermons I had recalled, as I so often have done, the story of their father Keane and I and our escape from the sea. I mentioned later that Keane didn't get saved until on the train trip back to Minnesota. The thought of their father in that stormy sea, not saved yet, and on the brink of death scared them so badly that they went home in tears.

"Their father wanted to know what was wrong, and they told him how scared it made them to think that he might have died without knowing the Lord Jesus as his Savior. Keane asked them if they knew the Lord. It stopped them cold as they looked at him, unsure if they did or not.

"Then, the most wonderful thing a parent can do for their child, he was able to have them each see that they were in as much danger as he had been. He told them that they weren't saved just because he and their mom were. They needed to make the decision for themselves, and that day Harmony did."

Jake smiled and reached out to pat Melody's hand. She smiled in return.

"Melody agreed with what her father said and for several years she thought she was saved. She asked me to tell you of the struggles she had in accepting her blindness and how angry she was with God for her condition, but it was Jasper who one day sat with her and helped her see—yes, I said *see*—the love God had for her despite her circumstances. He was able to help her truly make a decision to accept Christ. Melody and Jasper have shared a bond between them long before they agreed to stand here together to be joined as husband and wife."

"And then there's my nephew Garrett Prescott." Jake briefly told about Garrett's resistance to accepting salvation and how he finally made a decision as he came face to face with death.

"And now it is your turn, ladies and gentlemen. Getting saved isn't something you do, it's something you believe. If you have any questions, ask anyone here. We'll be glad to talk with you, but don't put it off. You don't know what tomorrow will bring. Let us pray."

The prayer ended and Tuva came to the front and stood between the two couples. Melody and Harmony turned to stand beside their mother and face the people. Together they blended their voices and sang:

> *Blessed assurance, Jesus is mine!*
> *O what a foretaste of glory divine!*
> *Heir of salvation, purchase of God,*
> *Born of His Spirit, washed in His blood.*

This is my story, this is my song,
praising my Savior all the day long;
this is my story, this is my song,
praising my Savior all the day long.

Then Jake began the ceremony and moments later the couples were married. "You may kiss your brides," Jake told the men. Then he announced to the people watching, "May I introduce to you, Mr. and Mrs. Ole Jasperson and Mr. and Mrs. Garrett Prescott."

Eddie jumped up from his seat beside Tuva and Keane. "That's my mom and dad!"

Everyone joined in the laughter as Jasper reached for the boy and had him walk down the aisle holding his hand and Melody's.

The well-wishers kept the couples busy through the rest of the afternoon and the meal. But finally it was time to go. Melody hoped for a moment alone with Harmony and was grateful when she appeared at her side.

They hugged. "Bye for now, Melody, or should I say Mrs. Jasperson?" Harmony's voice was filled with emotion. "I guess I've never told you, but I've always wanted to…to let you know how grateful I am that I got to be your eyes. You made me be aware of what was around me. I had to be, so I could later describe it to you. You made me see, Melody. You made me really see."

Tears were stinging Melody's eyes as she held her sister close. Her voice was shaky and she tried to laugh but it came out choked.

"I'm the one who's supposed to say that. Thank you, Harmony. You showed me the world around me. I am going to miss you so much." She wiped at her eyes. "Now, go be Mrs. Prescott, do great things, and come back and tell me every detail. Come back soon!"

"Love you!"

"Love you too!"

Jasper slipped his arm around his wife and she leaned back against him. "How did you know that was me, Mrs. Jasperson? Do you just cuddle up to anybody?"

Melody laughed and wiped the remainder of her tears away. She knew Jasper was helping her get over the tearful good-bye with Harmony, and she loved him for it.

"Ready to go?"

"I want to talk to Eddie first. Do you know where he is?"

"I'll find him." Soon Jasper was back and Eddie leaned against Melody's side.

"But I don't know why I can't go with you now. You're my mom and dad, aren't you? I don't want to stay with Grandpa and Grandma."

Melody knelt down and hugged her son. "I bet you forgot all about the surprise Grandpa has for you in the barn."

"That's right! I bet it's a horse! He's been teaching me to ride and I'm good at it." Then Eddie's voice dropped to a whisper. "Do you think it's a horse?"

"You'll have to go with him to find out. Just remember to act surprised, okay?"

"Okay. Bye. See you later." He was about to run off, but Jasper stopped him.

"No good-bye for me?"

Eddie threw his arms around Jasper's legs. "Bye, Dad. Love you."

Jasper chuckled as he drew Melody through the crowd to their buggy. "I hope we have a dozen just like him."

eighteen

One Year Later

Melody hummed as she put the last of the dishes away. Soon Jasper and Eddie would be in for lunch. The baby had been fed and the baking was done and put away. She was tired, but so happy. She listened with a smile on her face to the gentle snoring of Bear, the black Labrador Jasper surprised her with on her birthday. The big dog was as gentle as a kitten, but fiercely protective of his new family.

    The year had flown by, and she was finding it hard to believe that their anniversary was fast approaching. There had been struggles with Eddie as he learned his new environment, but he was quick and he wanted to learn. School was sometimes difficult. Well she remembered the trials she had faced, but Miss Emerson was still there and Naomi, at sixteen, had passed her teaching exams and was now her helper. Eddie loved Naomi.

Bear stood to his feet and Melody could hear his tail beat the wall as it wagged back and forth. She heard her men wipe their feet outside the door before they came in. She smiled at what a good father Jasper was. She and Eddie lived in a world of darkness, but Jasper was their light to what was around them. He never tired of explaining and describing things to them. He was almost as good at it as Harmony had been.

Melody sighed. She missed Harmony. The letters that came were full of news about the children's home and the progress that was being made. They had so much to do and had become involved in every aspect of the project. Garrett had gone to the businessmen in the city to raise donations to keep it funded and running for years to come. Harmony sounded happy and fulfilled in her new life, and Melody was happy for her, but she had never expected for them to be gone so long. They hoped to be home for Christmas, and Melody could hardly wait.

"Mmm! something smells mighty good in here, doesn't it, Eddie? Do you suppose Mom has made us some lapskaus?" Melody heard the lid being lifted off a pot. "Oh, no! It's lutefisk!"

Eddie was laughing. "No, it's not! If it was lutefisk, you'd be able to smell it in the barn." He sniffed. "It's stew, all right! You can't fool me!"

"Guess I can't. Well, we got by this time, but don't forget, Christmas will be coming and Grandma Wheatly loves to make lutefisk!" He grabbed for Eddie and tickled him until his giggling made all three of them laugh.

The baby cried then, and Jasper apologized over his shoulder to Melody as he hurried to get her. "Sorry about that, Mel. Guess we were too loud."

Melody shook her head. She knew full well that Jasper purposely woke Wilma up just so he could hold her. He came back to the dining room and she could hear him cooing and talking baby talk to the bundle in his arms.

"You know, I think she kind of looks like your Grandma Helma," he said. "It's a good thing we named her after her then."

"Wilma and Helma don't sound the same to me." Eddie insisted.

"My grandma's name was the same as Mina's. It was Wilhelmina. We just tried another variation of it for your sister."

"When will Wilma be big enough so I can play with her?"

"She needs to get a little bigger first, but you can hold her now if you want." Melody listened as Jasper positioned Eddie's arms to take the baby.

"I'm glad she's not blind too." he stated with childhood candor.

Melody smiled thoughtfully. It was the first question she had asked of her newborn daughter, but Jasper assured her that their baby had sight. Her heart was full of thankfulness.

"Someone's coming." Melody announced. Bear let out a low rumble.

Jasper looked up. "You always hear it before I do." He took Wilma from Eddie and went to the door. "I think it's just some mail being delivered."

"Mail? Why? Is it too big for Mr. Stende to leave in our box?"

"Much too big." Something in his voice made Melody stand up. "It's okay, Bear."

"Jasper, what's going on? Who's out there?" Melody began untying her apron. "How's my hair? Jasper, who is it?"

Melody could hear the door open and a gush of cold air rush into the room with the people who entered. She tried to keep a smile on her face though her eyebrows were drawn together in puzzlement. Why wasn't Jasper telling her who it was?

Then she heard Harmony's voice.

"Melody!"

Melody stood where she was and held out her arms. Soon Harmony was in them and they were hugging and laughing and crying and talking. Jasper clasped Garrett's hand a little awkwardly as they both had bundles in their arms.

"When did you get here? Are you staying? Have you been to see Mom and Dad?" The questions were pouring out of Melody until she felt Jasper's calming hand on her back and she quieted. "Come in, come in. Garrett, where are you? I need a hug."

"Thought you might like to hold your niece too while you're in a hugging mood. Say hello to Adele Tuva Prescott."

"Oh! Oh!" Melody had to sit down. "When? You never wrote to say…Harmony, a baby!"

A blanket was set in Melody's arms and she gently reached up and pulled it back. She stroked the tiny face inside and traced her features. "She has your nose," she commented.

At the same time Harmony was holding her niece and exclaiming over her. "They're only days apart, Mel. I didn't tell you because I wanted to surprise you and Mom and Dad. We're all invited over to their place for dinner, but I couldn't wait to see you. We had to come."

Lunch would have been forgotten had it not been for Jasper serving up bowls of stew and passing them out. The sisters talked steadily and the men caught up on their news. Melody finally remembered they were guests and wanted to serve coffee and dessert, but Harmony forestalled her.

"We'll all be together tonight for another visit, so I better get back to help Mom.

And Melody, we'll be here to stay. We'll have to go back to Chicago from time to time to see that things are being handled properly, but this is home now."

Melody couldn't contain her happiness. "It's so good to have you back!"

After they left, Melody set about to clean up the kitchen and to prepare some food to bring to her parents. Jasper came up and stood behind her. She lifted her head and smiled.

"I love you, Jasper."

"You always know where I am." He slid his arms around her and she leaned against him.

"I'm so happy."

"I'm glad."

"Harmony told me you asked them to come now. They were going to wait until Christmas." Melody turned to face Jasper.

"I couldn't have thought of a better anniversary gift to give you."

Melody pulled Jasper's face down to kiss him.

"Ole Jasperson, you do beat all."

References

Centennial Book Committee. *Spanning the Century–The History of Ulen, Minnesota 1886-1986.* Ulen, MN: *The Ulen Union*, 1985.

Crosby, Fanny J. *Blessed Assurance,* 1873. Melody by Phoebe Palmer Knapp. *Living Hymns,* Grand Rapids, MI: Zondervan Publishing House, 1967, p. 51. Public Domain.

Crosby, Fanny J. *All the Way My Saviour Leads Me,* 1875. Melody by Robert Lowry. *Living Hymns,* Grand Rapids, MI: Zondervan Publishing House, 1967, p. 407. Public Domain.

Newton, John. *Amazing Grace,* 1779. Unknown Author. *Verse 7*, 1829. *Living Hymns,* Grand Rapids, MI: Zondervan Publishing House, 1967, p. 385. Public Domain.

Raun, Agnes Lunde. *Pioneer Daughter-Memories of growing up on the prairies of Minnesota with my parents Swen and Ingeborg (Sylte) Lunde.* Complied by Eldora Lunde, 1993.

Roe, James. *Love Lifted Me,* 1912. *Living Hymns,* Grand Rapids, MI: Zondervan Publishing House, 1967, p. 390. Public Domain

75 Years of Progress-Ulen Diamond Jubilee 1886-1961. Ulen, MN, 1961.

Other books by Author Margo Hansen

A Newly Weds Series:
Sky's Bridal Train
Jade's Courting Danger
Emma's Marriage Secret
Irena's Bond of Matrimony
Mattie's Unspoken Vow

Tall Timber Trilogy:
Greatly Beloved
Only Beloved
Brother Beloved

A Sweet Voice

For more information about Author Margo Hansen:

www.margohansen.com

Margo would enjoy hearing from her readers.
Send your questions or comments to:

margo@margohansen.com

MARGO HANSEN, author of *A Newly Weds Series* and *Tall Timber Trilogy,* loves writing about the north woods of Minnesota where she lives with her husband Bruce. Her greatest desire is to share the Gospel of God's Grace with others through her stories.

Made in the
USA
Lexington, KY